Praise for
and her d 3 3

"Rose Pressey's books are fun!"
—*New York Times* best-selling author
Janet Evanovich

The Haunted Craft Fair Mystery Series
MURDER CAN MESS UP YOUR MASTERPIECE
"Plucky, self-employed heroine, cute pet, scary ghost,
and two eligible suitors: everything a cozy needs."
—*Kirkus Reviews*

"The paranormal twist adds a bit of flair to this
quirky new series."
—*The Parkersburg News & Sentinel*

The Haunted Vintage Mystery Series
IF YOU'VE GOT IT, HAUNT IT
"A delightful protagonist, intriguing twists, and a fash-
ionista ghost combine in a hauntingly fun tale. Definitely
haute couture."
—*New York Times* best-selling author Carolyn Hart

"If you're a fan of vintage clothing and quirky ghosts,
Rose Pressey's *If You've Got It, Haunt It* will ignite your
passion for fashion and pique your otherworldly interest.
Wind Song, the enigmatic cat, adds another charming
layer to the mystery."
—*New York Times* best-selling author
Denise Swanson

Books by Rose Pressey

The Haunted Craft Fair Mystery Series
Murder Can Mess Up Your Masterpiece
Murder Can Confuse Your Chihuahua
Murder Can Haunt Your Handiwork

The Haunted Vintage Mystery Series
If You've Got It, Haunt It
All Dressed Up and No Place to Haunt
Haunt Couture and Ghosts Galore
If the Haunting Fits, Wear It
Haunted Is Always in Fashion
A Passion for Haunted Fashion
Fashions Fade, Haunted Is Eternal

The Haunted Tour Guide Mystery Series
These Haunts Are Made for Walking
Walk on the Haunted Side
Haunt the Haunt, Walk the Walk
Walk This Way, Haunt This Way
Take a Haunted Walk with Me
Hauntin' After Midnight
Keep on Haunting
You'll Never Haunt Alone
The Walk That Haunts Me

The Halloween LaVeau Series
Forever Charmed
Charmed Again
Third Time's a Charm
Charmed, I'm Sure
A Charmed Life
Charmed Ever After
Once Upon a Charmed Time
Charmed to Death
A Charmed Cauldron
Almost Charmed

MURDER
Can Haunt Your Handiwork

Rose Pressey

KENSINGTON
PUBLISHING CORP.
www.kensingtonbooks.com

KENSINGTON BOOKS are published by

Kensington Publishing Corp.
119 West 40th Street
New York, NY 10018

All Kensington titles, imprints, and distributed lines are available at special quantity discounts for bulk purchases for sales promotion, premiums, fund-raising, and educational or institutional use.

Special book excerpts or customized printings can also be created to fit specific needs. For details, write or phone the office of the Kensington Sales Manager: Kensington Publishing Corp., 119 West 40th Street, New York, NY 10018. Attn. Sales Department. Phone: 1-800-221-2647.

The K logo is a trademark of Kensington Publishing Corp.

First Kensington Books Mass Market Paperback Printing: January 2021
ISBN-13: 978-1-4967-2165-5
ISBN-10: 1-4967-2165-9

ISBN-13: 978-1-4967-2166-2 (ebook)
ISBN-10: 1-4967-2166-7 (ebook)

10 9 8 7 6 5 4 3 2 1

Printed in the United States of America

To my father. I miss you, Dad. Every hour of every day.

CHAPTER 1

Travel Trailer Tip 1:
Always clean up your mess. You'll be happy
you did later, when you're busy investigating
a murder.

A loud crash echoed across the expanse of the massive room. Screams soon followed. Somehow, I knew the sounds were related to my brothers and/or my father. They were always in the middle of the chaos. If something destructive happened near them, then they were somehow typically involved.

I dashed around the corner and saw my brother Stevie standing behind the red velvet barrier rope. The space had been blocked off so that tourists would know to stay out. Either my brother chose to ignore the rope and the KEEP OUT warning signs, or he truly was clueless. Honestly, I thought he was just kind of oblivious. My brothers never meant harm. They just lived in their own little world.

My other brother, Hank, stood behind the rope barrier, too. Which one had knocked over the KEEP OUT sign? Fortunately, the large ceramic urn nearby, which I knew had to be an expensive piece of artwork, had survived the Cabot tornados. What did they think the KEEP OUT sign was there for, anyway? The piece had to be pricey and of significant importance, since it was featured on top of a pedestal column at the Biltmore Estate. Yes, my brothers were a walking disaster. It was no wonder, though. Their clumsiness combined with their muscular physiques made the right mix for disaster.

My family and I were currently touring the magnificent Biltmore mansion in Asheville, North Carolina. My family included my mother, father, grandmother, and two brothers. Now I questioned why I had agreed to come along with them for the tour. Obviously, I'd been wrong when I'd thought they could behave themselves, even for a short time.

My petite, gray-haired grandmother stood a good distance away from us, clinging to her brown pocketbook as if she might have to make a quick escape. Probably good thinking on her part. This wasn't her first rodeo with this bunch.

My mother clutched her pearl necklace as if the jewelry would save her from fainting. I'd picked out the necklace that my father had given her for their thirtieth anniversary. She'd pretended she believed he'd chosen the pearls, but she'd winked at me, indicating that she thought I'd made a perfect selection. Sometimes when I saw my mother, it was like seeing my own reflection. The resemblance was uncanny, since we both have dark hair and big brown eyes the shade of one of my favorite things—decadent chocolate.

"I don't know how I managed to get through over thirty years of this much chaos," my mother said.

My father was at a vintage car display. The sign recounted that the vehicle was rare, and there were only ten in existence.

"A 1913 Stevens–Duryea C-Six," my father said to no one in particular.

With the same strong stature as my brothers—although with a smidgen of added cushion—my father would inevitably get into trouble around breakables. As I watched in horror, he lifted the rope and scurried under to the other side. The extra weight around his middle made the movement harder than it would have been years ago, but he still managed to slide underneath.

"Mom!" I pointed.

"Oh, for Pete's sake, Eddie," she said as she ran over to him. "Get out from behind there before they arrest you."

"Why would they arrest me? They put the stuff here to enjoy, right?" My father reached out and grabbed an ornate vase, about two feet tall, painted with a colorful hunting scene.

Since I'd known him all my life, I understood what he'd said, but others had a hard time deciphering his low, mumbled words. Of course, as I feared, within seconds, the priceless piece slipped from my father's fingers. My mother dove for the item as if she were the star player in the baseball game trying to catch the ball. This all played out in slow motion. At least, that was the way it seemed in my mind. My mother caught the vase as she plunged to the floor. A groan escaped her lips as she rolled onto her side with the valuable antique still firmly in her arms. Gasps filled the once-silent room.

After catching her breath, my mother lifted the vase. "Got it!"

"Score," Hank yelled.

As my father helped my mother to her feet, I ran over and grabbed the vase before he had a chance to get his hands on it again.

Two employees, who had barely finished picking up after my brothers, raced over with stunned expressions on their faces. I kind of wanted to just run the other way, because I didn't want them to know I was involved. Since I now held the valuable piece of art, I supposed it would be hard to act as though I weren't related to these people. My brothers laughed from somewhere behind me. The male employee, whose grumpy expression seemed deeply etched into his florid face, flared his nostrils and marched over to me. His blue blazer with the Biltmore logo barely contained his hefty girth.

He yanked the vase from my arms. "Please step out from behind the rope."

His female companion, whose blue blazer hugged a slim figure, motioned for my mother and father to move, as well. Yes, a trip to the Biltmore Estate had definitely been a bad idea. What was once a lovely afternoon was now a complete disaster. I grabbed my brother Hank and pulled him to the side.

"What?" he said with a chuckle. "It was an honest mistake. Dad probably thought this was a flea market and was searching for a price tag."

"Why were you on the other side of that rope, too?" I asked. "I can't take you all anywhere."

"You never take me anywhere," he said.

"Now you know why," I said.

Yes, technically, my family had invited themselves on

this trip. They'd followed me all the way from Gatlinburg.

Stevie sauntered over to my side. "We just wanted to get a better view of the fancy-schmancy stuff. You can't blame us for that."

"Yes, I can blame you for that," I said in a louder voice than I'd intended.

A third employee joined our group. The word SECURITY was written in big white letters across the front of his black shirt. The tall, muscular, bald-headed man gestured toward the door. "We're going to have to ask you all to please exit."

"Oh no, I didn't get to see everything," my mother said in a pouty tone.

"Is it really necessary that we leave?" my father asked.

The man stared blankly at my father.

"He wants to know if it's necessary that we leave," I translated. "We'll be good."

The man gestured toward the door again, giving my father the answer without saying a word.

"Okay, I think it's best if we just go." I looped my arm through my mother's and guided her toward the door.

Glancing back, I realized my father was standing there, staring at the mural on the ceiling. I rushed over and yanked him with me. Everyone in the room stared at us. It was more attention than I wanted. My father and brothers reluctantly obeyed and marched behind us.

"Sorry," I said over my shoulder to the employees.

Frustration covered their faces, as if they wanted no part of my apology. I totally understood their point of view. Plus, my bank account couldn't afford reimbursing the estate if one of my wacky relatives broke something. Being asked to leave was a blessing in disguise.

My family and I walked past the groups of tour-goers entering the estate. They looked as if they were having a delightful time. With my family, I realized serenity wasn't in the cards for me. Bright sunshine surrounded us as we stepped out of the mansion. I blinked, trying to adjust to the light. A vast array of colors surrounded us—the lush lawns and trees full of green leaves. The assortment of trees included magnolia, cherry, and crabapple. Pink hyacinths, yellow daffodils, and red tulips bloomed around the space. It was so much to take in that I felt I'd never see it all.

"Well, thanks to you all, we almost got arrested," I said. "You should thank me for saving you from going to jail. Once again. It's like that time you all decided to work on Mr. Renfrow's car without telling him."

"We had to test-drive the Cadillac to see if it was fixed. If we'd told him, it would have ruined the surprise," Stevie said with an impish smile.

"I saved you from being arrested that time, too. Just like now," I said, pointing my finger.

"Why would you say that you saved us? What did we do?" Stevie asked with a frown.

"She got you out of there without causing any more damage," my mother said. "You all nearly broke something."

I motioned for my family to quicken their steps as we marched toward the parking area. With any luck, I'd convince them to go home. Not that I didn't love my family, but with their natural knack of creating chaos, I felt I owed it to everyone to keep them away. I was staying behind because I'd signed up to be a part of the Fifth Annual Fall Biltmore Estate Craft Fair being held right on the grounds. I couldn't have been happier about the up-coming event. If my family stayed, I knew something dis-astrous would happen. It would be like throwing a wet canvas tarp over my beautiful art.

I hoped to sell quite a few of my paintings while here. Each time I signed *Celeste Cabot* to the bottom of a painting, my heart danced. I took pride in signing my name to each one, since now I was full-time painter. Re-cently, I'd quit my job at my Aunt Patsy's diner back in Gatlinburg, Tennessee, and decided to chase my dreams. Never had I thought I'd have this opportunity. I knew it wouldn't be easy, but I was giving it my best shot.

As soon as my family left, I'd head over to the perime-ter of the estate, where the craft fair was to be held. To-morrow was the first day, and I had a lot to do before the first customers arrived. Not only did my paintings have to be ready, but I had to finish last-minute tasks, too. There was a lot more to a craft fair than just providing the items to sell.

"Well, goodbye, everyone, it's been a lot of fun." I gestured, shooing them away.

"She's being sarcastic now," Stevie said.

"You're right about that," I said.

"Don't be too mad at them, Celeste. They didn't mean to do anything," my mother said as she patted the backs of Stevie and Hank.

She was always defending them. That was partly why they acted this way. They were always getting into some-thing, and my mother ignored their behavior. My father was either accidentally setting fire to something or injur-ing himself, sometimes both. Stevie and Hank always broke things, including their bones. The anarchy would never end. One by one, I hugged them all and said good-bye.

"Thanks for coming, you all. I'll see you back at home," I said.

"Oh, we'll be back to help you later," my mother said with a smile. "Your father needs to eat and take a nap."

It was as if she were taking care of a toddler.

"What do you mean? Aren't you going back to Gatlinburg now?" I asked with panic in my voice.

Suddenly my chest felt tighter. My surroundings spun ever so slightly. It was hard to inhale. They hopped in my mom's blue Buick. My mother lowered the window.

"We'll be around tomorrow, dear. We haven't seen all of the estate, either. This is our vacation. See you." She held a glossy map of the grounds close to her face.

"Yeah, there's a lot more to do," Stevie said around a chuckle.

"Yes, we have to see more, I suppose," my father mumbled.

My family usually relayed my father's messages to others. Stevie and Hank smiled, and my father said something that I didn't understand this time. I suppose I wasn't one hundred percent fluent in his private language. I laughed to myself as the Buick pulled away with a slight squeal of the tires. Of course, people walking around the area all noticed when my family made their grand departure.

I wanted to hide behind the nearest pine tree. There was no time for that, however. They'd already scrutinized me, possibly wondering if I had an answer to why my family was so boisterous. I had no answer for that. Instead, I plastered a huge smile on my face, trying to indicate that everything was just peachy. At least I'd get a sliver of calm before the family storm returned. For now, I was on my way to my latest adventure. Nothing would wipe the smile from my face.

Even if I managed to convince my family to head home, I wouldn't be alone at the craft fair this week. I had my wonderful friend Vincent Van Gogh. My four-pound Chihuahua was my constant companion. I called him "Van" for short. People would say I rescued him from the shelter, but in reality, he had rescued me. I'd named him Van because he had one ear that flopped over, making it appear as if it were missing. Plus, my obvious love of art had spurred the moniker, too.

My 1947 pink Ford F-1 truck and my adorable pink-and-white Shasta trailer were parked just down the way. That was where I'd set up my art to sell tomorrow. Van was asleep in the trailer, waiting for me to return.

When I reached into my pocket, I realized my keys weren't there. Panic set in right away. Where had I lost them? This had better not be another of my brothers' practical jokes, like the time they stole my sneakers from gym class and I'd had to walk home barefoot. I had to find them soon, or I'd have to call a locksmith to open the trailer.

I bet I'd lost them inside the mansion. Would they allow me back inside to search for them? Probably not. Maybe they already had posters of my family plastered around with a NO ENTRY warning. Nevertheless, I had to try. I ran back over to the area where we'd been kicked out only a short time ago.

A middle-aged brown-haired woman stood at the door when I approached. She eyed me up and down. No doubt she recognized me.

I pulled out the ticket stub from my pocket. "I think I lost my keys inside. Do you mind if I go inside and check?"

She shrugged and motioned for me to go inside. I hadn't expected that. She didn't even so much as touch my ticket stub. I wouldn't mention this, though. If I pointed that out, she might change her mind. Once again, I hurried inside the mansion. People spoke in hushed tones in the distance. What would I do if the other employees recognized me? I suppose I'd deal with that when it happened.

With anxiety churning in my stomach, I walked down the hallway. I tried to keep my head held high, as if I were totally supposed to be here. I'd almost made it to the area where the vase incident happened. I figured this was the location where I'd lost the keys. As I headed farther down the hall, a piercing scream rang out. What had happened? Had my family returned? That wasn't possible, right? The next thing I knew, a stampede of people raced toward me. I dove to my left so that I wouldn't be trampled.

I landed face first on the floor but not before knocking down one of those velvet rope barriers that I had just chastised my brothers about being behind. I briefly remained motionless, dazed and wondering what had just happened. The crowd thundered by like a herd of cattle without saying a word to me. Apparently, they just wanted out.

I managed to get up from the floor. After straightening my clothing and smoothing down my frazzled hair, I picked up the gold posts holding the barrier rope. Curiosity got me, and I really wanted to take a peek around the corner and see what the crowd could've possibly been running from. I didn't smell smoke, nor did I hear a fire alarm. What other emergency could there have been? One quick glance around the corner, and I saw the motionless woman on the floor.

CHAPTER 2

Travel Trailer Tip 2:
Plan ahead and have an emergency contact
list. It will help you keep calm in case of
murder.

Was this some kind of stunt? Like one of those murder-mystery theaters? I stared in disbelief at the body. The woman's cinnamon-sugar-colored hair was pulled back into a ponytail. She wore the estate's uniform of navy-blue pants, a crisp white shirt, and a navy vest.

When the woman didn't move, I realized this was no joke. I had to help her. Why had everyone run in the opposite direction? I ducked under the velvet barrier rope that was blocking my entrance and raced across the floor toward her. Once I reached the woman, I saw the bluish color of her face, and I knew this was urgent.

"Are you all right?" I asked, already knowing the answer.

She didn't respond. I knelt down beside her body to check for any signs of life. I pressed my fingertips against her neck and soon realized she had no pulse. My heart beat faster as I pulled my phone from my pocket. I had to call for help.

"Place your hands in the air and don't move," a male voice said from somewhere behind me.

Oh no. Now I needed help for myself. And I complained about my brothers getting into trouble. Apparently, I was just as bad as them. The apple didn't fall far from the tree.

Doing as I was told, I stuck my hands in the air with the phone still in my hand. Thank goodness I'd already placed the 911 call. The operator's voice sounded from above my head, asking if I needed police, ambulance, or firefighters. I wasn't sure what I needed; possibly a lawyer. The next thing I knew, a uniformed police officer came over to me and instructed me to place my hands behind my back. Was this really happening? He placed me in handcuffs. The cold metal was loose around my wrists. Could I slip out of these things?

Lucky for me, my brothers weren't around to see this. They would talk about this nonstop. As a matter fact, when they found out, they would still talk about it nonstop. It would be a laughing matter to them. But if they were visiting me in prison, I wasn't sure I would be laughing. My brothers would recount this story at every Christmas gathering. The police officer pulled me to my feet as other uniformed men raced toward us.

"What's your name?" asked the dark-haired officer, who appeared barely old enough to drive, in a stern voice.

I'd never been in trouble with the law. Other than the time my cousin's best friend's sister was caught shoplifting candy and they made us all wait until her parents arrived. That was when I was eight years old. Twenty-five years later, and I'd managed to stay out of trouble until now. Not even a speeding ticket.

"Celeste Cabot," I said with a trembling voice.

"What happened here, Ms. Cabot?" he asked.

"I had nothing to do with this," I said, wiggling my arms. "You have to believe me."

I tried to stay calm so that I wouldn't hyperventilate.

He held up his hand. "All right, Ms. Cabot, just calm down. Tell me what happened."

After releasing a deep breath, I said, "I came back in here to find my keys that I'd lost. When everyone ran at me like a stampede, I tumbled to the floor. They all took off. I checked to see what had caused the chaos, and I saw the woman on the ground. I was merely offering assistance. I would never harm anyone, ever."

He studied my face as if trying to determine if I were being truthful. I hoped he came to the right decision, because I was being one hundred percent honest with him.

"And you don't know this woman?" he asked.

"Not at all. I assume she works here based on the uniform, but other than that, I know nothing about this. I was trying to call 911."

The call had obviously dropped at this point, but I gestured for him to check the phone.

"Are you just here for the day?" he asked.

"I'm part of the craft fair that's in town. I have a couple of law enforcement friends. They can vouch for me," I said. "Their names are Caleb Ward and Pierce Meyer."

The young officer's face registered his surprise. "Pierce is your friend?" he asked.

"Yes, we're friends. Do you know him?"

"We're good friends," he said with a hint of a smile that revealed his dimples.

What a lucky break. Maybe now he would let me go.

"Just ask him. I'm on the up and up," I said.

Sure, I could be a little quirky at times, but I believed Pierce would vouch for me. The officer reached around and unlocked the handcuffs. My quickened heartbeat steadied a touch as I realized that I wouldn't be escorted out of the Biltmore Mansion in handcuffs.

"I will check with Pierce," he said.

"Absolutely," I said.

"And you're not going anywhere or leaving town, right?"

"No, I have the craft fair. As long as the craft fair is continuing, now that there's been a death. How did she die?" I asked.

I hated to admit it, but it didn't seem as if this were a natural death, accident or self-inflicted. Foul play had to be involved.

"Wait a minute. You said you lost your keys. Did you find them?" he asked.

"Actually, no," I said.

I cringed at what he must be thinking.

"Is that right?" he asked.

"I haven't found my keys yet," I said.

"But you know you lost them inside?" His words dripped with skepticism.

"Yes, at least I think so," I said.

I scanned the marble floor, and instant relief washed over me when I spotted my keys. They were right in the spot where we'd had the vase incident. The officer followed my gaze.

"I'll just pick them up," I said, stepping forward.

He stopped me. "I'll get them."

I froze on the spot and allowed him to pick up the

keys. He turned them over in his hand as if searching for a clue on them. Did he think he'd find blood or some- thing? I hoped he didn't slap the handcuffs back on me.

After a few agonizing seconds, he handed me my keys back. "I'm still going to talk to Pierce."

"Yes, I hope that you will," I said.

I was kind of getting upset now, because I honestly had nothing to do with this. I felt like it should be some- what evident. Just because I'd been in the room with the woman, hovering over her dead body, didn't mean that I had actually killed her. By now, I was pretty sure her death was a murder.

"I hope you know that I'm not making this up. I really lost my keys," I said.

He gave me a skeptical look. Maybe I should stop talk- ing. It seemed like the more I said, the worse I made this for myself. It didn't help that other officers in the room were eyeing me as if I were guilty. At least that was the way I felt. Maybe it was just me being paranoid.

A pair of familiar male voices caught my attention. Pierce and Caleb appeared in the hallway. We all made eye contact, and I grimaced. They stepped into the room and walked toward me. Talk about handsome . . . each man was a tall glass of water. Pierce, with his raven- colored hair, ever-changing hazel eyes, and chiseled fea- tures, had a mysterious edge. Caleb had caramel-colored hair with streaks of light blond; his eyes as blue as a cloud- less summer day, which always made me happy. Had they coordinated their outfits today? Both men wore khaki pants and white Polo shirts. I'd been so accustomed to seeing Pierce in a suit, I found it a strange to see him dressed somewhat casually.

Both men were in law enforcement, so it was no surprise to see them at the scene. However, this wasn't their jurisdiction. The two had a rivalry that I had yet to explain. It seemed as if they were getting along just fine right now, though. Possibly because they'd heard I was involved in some kind of incident. They hurried over to me.

"Celeste, what's going on?" Pierce asked.

"I found the woman," I said. "I came back in to find my keys, and there she was on the floor. Everyone else had left her, so I had to do something."

"Excuse me, Pierce, but may I speak with you?" The dark-haired officer wiggled his index finger, gesturing for Pierce to come closer.

Pierce stepped away with the officer, leaving me alone with Caleb.

"Are you all right?" Caleb asked.

I blew the hair out of my eyes. "Yes, I'll be fine. It was certainly shocking. I just can't believe this happened. At first, they thought I had something to do with it. I still think they might be suspicious."

"Well, that's only natural, considering there was a body found, and they caught you standing over it."

I winced. "You heard about that, huh?"

"Yes, I heard about it," he said.

Caleb and Pierce were here for the arts and crafts fair. Caleb and I had met at another craft fair in Gatlinburg. He'd been working undercover, but he was quite a good artist, too. Pierce had mysteriously taken up art recently. I was suspicious that he might have done it so that he could come to the craft fair, too; then Caleb and I wouldn't be alone here. If that were true, it was awfully sweet.

Caleb and I had gone on several dates. We had quite a good amount in common, since we both were into art and both of us had dogs. Caleb had an adorable German Shepherd named Gum Shoe. But Pierce was smart and handsome, and surprisingly, he had a sense of humor when he wasn't being the tough cop.

"What happens next?" I asked. "Will they drag me away to the slammer?"

"As far as I know, you're not going to the slammer." Caleb used air quotes. "What do you mean by 'what happens next'?"

"How will they find who did this to her? Will the fair continue?"

"First, they have to confirm that it was a homicide. Second, I assume the fair will continue. They'll probably try to act as if nothing happened," Caleb said.

A photographer from the police department was snapping photos, making flashes of bright light in rapid succession. Occupancy in the room had swollen, and now I was feeling claustrophobic. I had to get out of here soon.

"I think we can safely assume that it was murder," I said as I pulled at the neck of my T-shirt. With every passing second, I found it harder to breathe.

"Oh no. I can see the amateur sleuth wheels turning in your head. Maybe it would be a good idea if you didn't get involved," Caleb said.

"Not get involved? Not get involved?" I gestured widely with my hand. "I have to get involved now. I'm practically a detective on the case now. After all, I was the first one on the scene. That means I have to get involved."

"Wait just a minute," Pierce said.

I hadn't realized that he had stepped beside me.

"There are plenty of detectives here to handle the case,

and I think they have everything under control," Pierce added.

"Pierce is right. They can handle this, Celeste," Caleb said.

Now they were agreeing with each other? I would humor Caleb and Pierce and act as if I weren't getting involved, but I knew I would. Seeing the woman like that just made me want to help her. It was heartbreaking. We had to know who did this to her. I had faith in the detectives, of course, but I was sure they could use some help. Who couldn't use help every now and then?

Caleb and Pierce stared at me suspiciously. I had to pretend that I agreed with them.

"Okay, I guess you guys are right," I said with a smile.

Did that seem genuine? I needed to work on my acting skills.

"I think it's time we got you out of here," Caleb said, taking me by the arm.

Pierce took my other arm. "Yes, that's a good idea."

Now I was being escorted out of the building. This wouldn't look good, either. At least I wasn't in handcuffs. Being escorted by two handsome men wasn't so terrible. Though the rivalry between them was getting out of control.

When we stepped out into the bright sunshine, Pierce and Caleb released their hold on me. I shielded my eyes until they adjusted to the light. A crowd had gathered just beyond the taped-off area. News crews had arrived. Several vans, with their stations' call letters written across the sides, were parked close by. Since the reporters' attention was focused on us as we walked toward them, I knew we would be bombarded with questions.

"Just tell them 'no comment'," Pierce said.

"This doesn't sound good. Why do I have to say 'no comment'? I had nothing to do with this," I said.

"Nevertheless, they'll ask questions." Pierce projected an air of confidence that I hoped I could emulate.

"You don't want to give them information that might jeopardize your case, right?" Caleb asked with a wink.

I scoffed. "Now you're just mocking me."

He chuckled. "Just trying to help."

"I'm glad you're getting amusement out of this, both of you," I said.

They could poke fun all they wanted. I'd show them. I stood tall and pushed my shoulders back as we marched toward the crime scene tape. I couldn't let this rattle me.

"Are you the one who found the body?" a dark-haired woman yelled as we crossed the tape.

How did she know? They found this stuff out so quickly. Someone must have blabbed. At least she hadn't asked if I'd killed the woman. I didn't even reply with a "no comment." Instead, I didn't utter a word. I kept my focus straight ahead. Smooth and confident, just like Pierce.

A couple other newspeople pushed microphones in my face. Caleb and Pierce shooed them away. I was proud of how calm I remained. I just wanted to escape the scene and get back to the safe haven of my trailer. I wanted to see Van. Perhaps I needed to leave the area for a while until all of this settled down. Chocolate cake was definitely called for. How would I tell my family about this? Could I keep it from them forever? Probably not. They had a way of finding things out. I had no idea how they did it.

"Great job back there," Pierce said.

Really? He'd noticed? I pushed my shoulders back. I knew I'd handled that well.

"Thank you," I said. "I thought I did pretty good."

"No matter what they do or how much they sneak around, don't give in to them. Don't tell them anything," Pierce warned.

This sounded serious. Would I be able to stand strong? What if I slipped up? The reporters watched us as if plotting their next move.

I gave a salute. "Yes, sir."

I tried to act nonchalant, as if I had everything under control. Now I had to keep it up, though, and not show a crack in my armor.

"Just don't get involved," Pierce and Caleb said in unison.

Had they been practicing?

"You got it," I said, giving a thumbs-up.

CHAPTER 3

Travel Trailer Tip 3:
It's nice to have visitors, but try to keep
guests to a minimum. There's just not enough
room for a party in a travel trailer.

Back at my trailer, I sat inside on the sofa/bed with Van on my lap. He dozed while I replayed the morning's events in my head. The craft fair had been postponed for a day, but not canceled. Therefore, I had extra time on my hands.

At least I had the cozy surroundings of my safe haven. I loved my pink-and-white retro trailer, but the space was small. Cramming my paints, brushes, canvases, and easel into the corner meant that I'd brought only the essentials. Luckily, at the back of the trailer, the benches and table fit tightly into the space and converted into a bed. A pink-and-white quilt, along with several toss pillows my grandmother made me, covered the top of the bed. One pillow had pink hearts, and the others were pink gingham.

The storage area installed to the back of my trailer allowed me to haul more paintings for the craft fair. Showing their sweet side, my brothers had installed the storage area and painted it in the exact shade of pink to match my trailer.

My thoughts turned back to the crime. Who was the woman who had been murdered? Of course, from her uniform, I knew she was a tour guide for the estate, but I wanted to know her name. I wanted to know all about her. How would I figure out who had murdered her unless I knew about her life?

My theory was that this wasn't a random act. Plus, it probably wasn't premeditated, considering there were so many people around. The murderer wouldn't want to take a chance on being caught unless they hadn't planned this out.

That meant the killer had decided to carry out this act at the spur of the moment. I had to figure out who to ask about this woman. Obviously, other employees of the estate would know her, so I would probably start there. I wasn't sure if I would be able to get information from the police. Considering neither Caleb nor Pierce would be investigating this crime, I wouldn't have an inside source. Not that they would share anything with me, anyway.

In my opinion, the likely cause of death had been strangulation, since she had the velvet rope wrapped around her neck. That meant that the murderer hadn't brought a weapon with them to the scene. Which further verified my theory that she had been murdered by someone in a crime of passion. Perhaps a boyfriend or jealous friend?

Since the craft fair had been delayed for a few hours, I had some extra time to perhaps start my investigation. However, there was something else on my mind. I groaned when I saw the number pop up on my phone. Not that I didn't love talking to my grandmother, but I knew she'd sense something in my voice. I'd have to confess the day's events. My secret wouldn't last long.

"Hello, Grammy," I said when I answered.

My voice wavered. I knew it. She hesitated, and I knew she sensed the problem already. Nothing got past her.

"What's wrong?" she asked.

"What do you mean?" Why was I even trying with this act? It was pointless.

"How many years have I known you now?" Grammy asked.

"All of them that I've been alive," I said.

"Which is exactly why you should know that I'm not falling for your innocent act. Now, I can tell by the tone of your voice that something is wrong, so you might as well tell me now and save me the hassle of having to figure it out on my own."

I released a lungful of air. "Have you watched the local news?"

"Are you injured?" she asked in a panic. "What happened? Did someone harm you? I know it can't be your brothers, because they're here at the hotel with me."

"No one injured me," I said.

"I'm listening," she continued.

"Well, there was a murder at the estate a short time ago."

"Oh, land's sake," she said.

"I don't know for sure that it was a murder yet, but it seemed like a murder to me," I said.

"What makes you think it was a murder? Exactly how close were you to the murdered person?" Grammy asked.

"I discovered her body," I blurted out.

"Oh, for land's sake," Grammy said again.

"And the police may have handcuffed me for a short time. But they let me go because of Pierce and Caleb. The police thought I actually did it, Grammy."

"Well, the very idea," she said. "They better never put my grandbaby in handcuffs again. I'll tell them a thing or two."

I pictured her shaking her fist.

"Okay, calm down, Grammy. Everything is fine now."

This was part of the reason why I didn't want to tell her. It would get her blood pressure up too much. I didn't want to be responsible for causing Grammy to have a stroke.

"I'm on my way there right now, as soon as I get my pocketbook," she said.

"Grammy, no, wait, it's not necessary for you to come over here. Everything is fine."

"How can you say everything is fine when they almost took you to the slammer?"

"See, that's the thing, they didn't take me. That's why everything is fine." I checked out the trailer window to see if any reporters lurked around.

"You should thank your lucky stars for Caleb and Pierce. Those are two fine men. And I mean that in more ways than one."

"Grammy!" I said.

She laughed. "We're still coming over there to get you."

"Not until the designated time, remember? You know I don't want chaos here. It's like bringing a tornado with you."

"I understand. Your brothers and father can be a handful, but they really are only trying to help."

"It's like asking a bull to help display the china in the cabinet."

She giggled. "I see your point, dear, but you know I have to tell your mother, and she'll want to come over right away, too."

"Why do you have to tell her?"

"You know I don't keep anything from her."

"That's not true," I said. "You didn't tell her when you didn't eat that cake she baked for you. In fact, you told her that it was delicious."

"Well, bless her heart, that one didn't turn out so well. It was as dry as a pack of saltines."

"Nevertheless, I think you should just wait, okay?" I asked.

Silence filled the line.

"Hello? Grammy?"

Pulling the phone away from my ear and checking the screen, I saw that the call had ended. Oh no. Grammy had already set the wheels of that crazy family train in motion.

I dialed her number again. No answer. Grammy had me on ignore. Grandmothers always answered calls. Grammy would have maneuvered an obstacle course like a ninja warrior to answer my call. Before I had a chance to hit redial, my phone rang. Oh no. My mother's number. Apparently I was losing this battle. What made me think I'd win against a competitor like Grammy? I might as well take the call and get this over with. Maybe there was still a way to stop them from coming over.

"I assume Grammy is standing right next to you with her pocketbook?" I asked when I answered.

"She's motioning for us to get in the Buick."

It was too far gone.

"Can I convince you to let me come there? I'm leaving right now," I said.

My mother hesitated. "Are you being honest?"

"You'd find out soon enough if I was lying, and I'd be in even bigger trouble with you all, so what's the point of not telling the truth now?"

"All right, Celeste. How long will it take you to get here? Is it safe for you to leave your trailer?" she asked.

"This is not a hostage situation, Mom," I said. "The killer isn't lurking outside my trailer waiting for me."

"How do you know that?" she asked.

My mother had a way of making everyone paranoid. Better safe than sorry, she'd say.

"It wasn't a random attack. Listen, I'll be there in fifteen minutes."

"I'll be watching the clock," she said.

I knew she meant that. How would I get my painting done before going to see them? I knew I couldn't waste any time. I needed to get out of there right away. I dressed Van in his little blue sport shirt and gathered a few of his toys and dishes into my bag. Peeking out the door, I checked to see if anyone was around. After the warning from Pierce and Caleb, I had to be on guard for the reporters, I supposed. The coast seemed clear, so I stepped out of the trailer and locked the door behind me.

No one seemed to pay any attention to me as they busied themselves getting ready for the show. I was proud of myself that I was already prepared. All I had to do was set out my paintings. With Van in my arms, I hurried over to my truck parked just around the way.

After unloading the trailer, I'd moved my truck out to the parking lot, because it would have taken up too much room. Space between each booth was limited so that they could fit in as many vendors as possible. I'd just turned the ignition when I received a text message. Caleb asked if I was all right. That was sweet.

Everything is good. I added a smiley-face emoji.

My phone dinged again. This time, it was a text from Pierce, asking exactly the same thing. They were so competitive. I wasn't sure how they knew, but they each had sent the exact message. I responded with the same answer, even adding the smiley face.

"Remember, don't talk to reporters," Caleb had said.

That reminded me to check around again. Reporters could be hiding behind trees, lurking in a nearby car. I glanced through the back window to make sure no one was in the bed of my truck. All seemed clear. I tossed my phone back into my bag. Pulling out of the parking lot, I headed away from the estate to meet my family. The drive to the hotel was a short distance away.

My mother had wanted to know why I wouldn't just stay at the hotel with them. I told her why spend the money when I had a perfectly good trailer to stay in? Though I had to admit, part of the reason why was that I knew there would be much chaos with them. I loved my family more than anything, but I could only be around them in small doses.

As I sat at a red light, I noticed a cute little bakery to the left. A pink-and-white-striped awning hung over the door, with a big sign above bearing the name SWEET TOOTH. Too bad I didn't have time to stop now. The drawing of the giant cupcake on the window made me crave a chocolate cupcake. I liked my cupcakes the best, though. I used my grandmother's recipe, and they always came out moist and rich. I'd have to remember this bakery for later.

The light turned green, and I headed down the street.

After traveling a short distance, I noticed a black car behind me. It was trailing me awfully close. I couldn't see exactly who was behind the wheel, because the person wore big black sunglasses. Based on the long blond hair spilling out from under the baseball cap and the large gold hoop earrings, I guessed this was a woman. Maybe she was just a bad driver.

With the car so near, my anxiety grew, and a gnawing dread pulled at my stomach. I pushed on the gas pedal just a touch. Unfortunately, so did the woman behind the wheel. Now I was panicking for sure. I had to get away from her. What did she want? Could this be a reporter? Well, if she thought she was going to get a scoop from me, she was sadly mistaken.

I swung an immediate left and pushed on the gas more. A traffic light was up ahead. I hoped it didn't catch me.

"Stay green, stay green," I said.

She had turned onto the street, as well. Now I was certain she was following me. What made it even worse was that I had no idea where I was headed. I didn't know this town's streets, and I could easily get lost. That could turn into a dangerous situation quickly.

Perhaps I should stop and confront this woman. I'd tell her to leave me alone. She would probably get that on video, and this would become even worse. No, I should just try to get away from her. For all I knew, the press would say that I was running from them and unwilling to talk about what happened. I was getting ahead of myself.

These were all worst-case scenarios and probably nothing close to what would actually happen. Nevertheless, I wanted to get away from her. The more I pushed the accelerator, the more she did, too. Lucky for me, I zoomed right through the green light. That brought little relief, though. Now I was nearing a congested area. There would be no way I would get away from her now.

I noticed an upcoming street and knew I had to make that turn so I wouldn't be stuck in traffic. It came up so soon that I had little warning. Whipping the steering wheel to the right, I made the quick turn, squealing my tires as my pink truck maneuvered the street.

I thought about trying to hide my truck somewhere, but it was kind of tough to conceal a pink truck. I might as well have a big neon flashing sign on the back of the truck that read FOLLOW ME. There were a few restaurants and stores up ahead, so possibly I could whip into a parking lot and hide. However, I was sure the pursuer was focused on me like a laser, and it wouldn't be that easy to get away from her.

I wished there were more traffic so that I could maneuver between cars and possibly lose her. One good thing about having my father teach me to drive was now I had skills like a NASCAR driver. Although the other drivers probably didn't appreciate it much. The good part of my skills was that as I drove, I was conscientious of other drivers, something that the person following me was lacking. It seemed as if she didn't care if she ran other cars off the road or caused an accident. Someone might call the police and report her soon.

Out of nowhere, a siren blared, and twirling blue lights appeared behind me. Just when I thought my day couldn't get any worse. Someone had called the cops, all right, but they apparently had reported me instead of her. That hardly seemed fair. Now I was being pulled over by the police. Two encounters with the cops in one day. What would Caleb and Pierce say? No doubt they would disapprove.

My family would probably send out a search party for me, considering it shouldn't take me this long to arrive at the hotel. The text messages and phone calls would start soon. I had hoped that the police officer wasn't trying to pull me over, but as he trailed along right behind me, I knew that wasn't the case.

After merging to the side of the street, I pulled out my driver's license and vehicle registration. Wait. What if this wasn't a stop for reckless driving? What if this was when the police arrested me for murder? My chest tightened as I struggled to breathe, as if someone had placed a plastic bag over my head. Even my arms and hands tingled. Hyperventilating. Yes, that was happening. They'd have to call an ambulance for me soon. Obviously, I didn't handle stress well.

Should I put my hands up or keep them on the wheel? The decision had to be made in a split second. Keeping them on the wheel seemed like the best option. I didn't want the officer to think that I automatically assumed I was being arrested for murder. That would mean I thought I was guilty. I rolled the window down and waited for him to approach. He still hadn't gotten out of his car. What was he waiting for? This was torture. I had to know why I was being stopped.

CHAPTER 4

In reality, it was probably only thirty seconds before the officer climbed out from behind the wheel. Slowly, he approached my truck. It was like watching a snail crawl up a leaf. One slow step at a time. I thought for sure I'd seen the black car pull over, too, after making the turn behind the police officer. I thought the woman had parked behind a few cars at the end of the street behind me.

Had this officer been at the estate when I'd found the victim? Would he remember me from being involved in the earlier incident at the estate? I suppose he was just assigned to traffic patrol and not a death investigation.

One positive thing about being stopped was maybe now the woman would stop following me. I hope she didn't find me again when I took off—if the officer allowed me to leave. Maybe I should tell the police officer I was being followed, and that was why I had been speeding.

However, considering she was nowhere in sight now, I had nothing to prove that it had actually happened. My story might cause more harm than good, so I'd just let it go. The officer, who had honey-blond cropped hair, was beside the truck now. My gaze traveled to the utility belt around the waist of his perfectly pressed blue uniform, which included a gun, baton, radio, and handcuffs. Was that a stun gun? From the scowl on his face, I gathered he was not happy with me. At least he hadn't told me to get out and put my hands behind my back. But I wouldn't release a sigh of relief just yet.

"Hello, officer," I said with a shaky voice.

I would say nothing else. I would admit no guilt.

"Going somewhere in a hurry?" He peered at me over the top of his mirrored sunglasses.

"As a matter of fact, I was trying to get away from that car that was chasing me."

I groaned. I wished I hadn't said that.

He removed the sunglasses. "A car was chasing you?"

I chuckled. "Well, I guess I thought the person was. They were probably just tailgating. Maybe I've been watching too many crime shows."

For heaven's sake, couldn't I just keep my mouth shut? Now I had mentioned crime. The more I talked, the more suspicious I sounded. Since I couldn't read his expression, I didn't know if the handcuffs were getting ready to come out.

He studied my face. "Have I seen you before?"

Why would he say that? Had I been on the news? Oh my gosh. I bet my face had been plastered on the morning news already. I needed to check. No doubt my hair and makeup had been a mess. Why worry about that, though? If I went to jail, I doubted my beauty routine would be a top priority.

"Well, I'm not from around here, officer," I said, trying to sound casual. "Maybe it's someone with similar features. Perhaps a sweet next-door neighbor or polite woman you met at the post office. You know, totally innocent things?"

What was I rambling about? Did I want him to take me to jail? If so, I was certainly on the right track. *Shut up now, Celeste.*

He looked at my driver's license, studying it for way too long. In my defense, it had been a bad hair day, and the woman snapped the photo way too soon. Yes, one eye was open and one eye closed, as if I'd been winking. I had no idea how it was even possible to get a photo that bad, but somehow, I'd managed. My brothers had gotten hold of my driver's license and had a poster made of it. They'd used it to decorate my surprise twenty-fifth birthday party two years ago. The renewal time for my license couldn't come fast enough.

After studying the picture, he focused on me again. "I know where I saw you."

Now came the time when I would be arrested. I might as well get it over with and place my hands behind my back. How embarrassing that I'd be shoved into the back of the police cruiser.

"You were the one who found the murdered woman at the Biltmore Estate," he said.

I sucked in air and exhaled. "Yes, that was me. I didn't kill her. Obviously, they didn't arrest me, so that means I'm not a murderer."

"I didn't say you were a murderer." He handed me the driver's license back. "But you might want to slow down, considering."

Considering that I had someone chasing me? He should arrest the woman who was following me. I glanced in the rearview mirror to see if the car was still back there. I wasn't sure, but I thought I saw it. Maybe I could convince him to go back there and question her. Yeah, that was unlikely to happen.

Now I was just rambling again and telling him exactly what happened at the estate. He was patiently listening to me, but it was almost as if he were thinking, "You're guilty." He probably didn't even want to hear my side of the story. Clearly, the reporters wanted to hear, though. His skeptical expression made me wonder why he hadn't slapped the handcuffs on me.

"So that's what happened," I said.

The officer thrust my registration back. My hand shook as I took it from him.

He eyed me and then said, "I'll be right back."

I watched as he walked away from my truck. Oh, great. Now what was happening? I thought he was on his radio back there. I couldn't handle much more of the stress. I needed to get out of here. I was starting to become claustrophobic in my own truck. After a couple minutes, he got out of the car and slowly walked toward my truck.

The officer was a little scary and intimidating. He walked up to the driver's side window again. After my rambling story, he probably thought I was certifiable.

"I'm sorry, but I had to write you a ticket for speeding." He scribbled something on the pad in his hand.

After I'd had a rough day already, this certainly didn't

help. Discovering a dead woman apparently was only the start to my bad luck. The dead woman had a much worse day than me, though, so who was I to complain? Now it seemed like a good thing to get a ticket. I would gladly take that over being murdered. Plus, it was much better than going to jail.

Just as the police officer handed me the ticket, my phone rang. And it just kept ringing. As soon as the chiming stopped, it would start back up again. The calls were either from my mother or my grandmother. Soon, the police officer would get a call for a missing-persons case, and he'd be standing right next to the so-called missing person. A pink truck was kind of hard to miss, too.

"Do you need to get that call?" he asked.

"Oh no, it's just my mother or grandmother." I chuckled. "They probably think I've been murdered."

He rapidly blinked a few times. I'd said 'murdered' again. Could I stop talking about that now? Every time I opened my mouth, the wrong words spewed out.

I chuckled nervously again. "After finding a body, they think the killer is still out there and might come after me."

"Well, obviously the killer is still out there . . ." he said matter-of-factly.

Great. He'd focused on me like a laser when he said that. Did that mean he thought I did it? We'd been through this before. I was not the killer.

"I found the body, and now they think the killer possibly wants to find me, thinking that I saw what happened."

"That's a distinct possibility. You never know if the perpetrator might come after you. One minute you're here, and the next you're a goner," he said with a click of his tongue.

I should have thanked him for making me feel better, and I meant that in the most sarcastic way possible. As if I weren't worried enough. I was glad my grandmother and mother weren't here to hear him say all that.

"Now make sure to slow down," he said.

"Yes, officer," I said.

I didn't even bother to check the ticket to find out how much that would cost. There went my profit from sales this weekend. And all because someone had been chasing me. That didn't seem quite fair, either. Unfortunately, life wasn't always fair.

My phone continued to ring. I couldn't answer right now, either, because I would get a ticket for that, too. I'd have to pull over the first chance I got. With the woman following me, though, I wasn't sure when I'd have the opportunity. I just wanted the officer to stop trailing me, too. He remained parked behind me, and I felt like he wanted me to drive first, so I merged my truck back onto the road, paying special attention to do exactly the speed limit. Not too fast and not too slow.

I spotted a restaurant up ahead and decided to pull over into the parking lot so that I could make the constant ringing stop. Putting on the turn signal, I slowly steered into the lot. When I parked the truck, the cop drove on by.

"Mother," I yelled when I answered the phone.

"Oh, thank God you answered. Why didn't you answer your phone? We were ready to call the police."

"I know you were ready to call the cops. No need, though, because I was talking to one while you were constantly calling," I said in frustration.

"Oh, you were talking to Caleb or Pierce? I'm sure they would have wanted you to answer a call from your dear, sweet mother."

"No, I wasn't talking to Caleb or Pierce."

"Were you being arrested for murder? I knew it! I can't breathe. It's okay, honey, we'll get you the best lawyer we can afford. Never mind your father and I were saving for a cruise. I'm sure we'll get another chance to see Greece."

My mother had a natural knack for making people feel guilty. It wasn't always subtle, though.

"No, I was not arrested for murder," I said.

"Oh, good. Greece is still on, Eddie," she yelled.

"I was getting a speeding ticket, and I couldn't answer your calls. It's really not necessary to call a million times."

"Well, excuse me, but I was just wondering if I was having to plan your funeral."

That wasn't dramatic at all.

"I'm on my way right now. I'm like two minutes away," I said.

"All right, dear," she said in a calm voice, as if everything were perfectly fine.

Pulling out onto the street, I kept an eye out for the mystery car. I also watched for a police officer. I hoped speeding wouldn't be necessary this time. I made it to the hotel. When I wheeled into the parking lot, my whole family was outside waiting. My brothers paced across the hotel's entrance. With droopy eyes and tousled hair, my father leaned against the building, giving the impression that he'd just woken up from a nap.

Grammy stood by the hotel's door with her big brown pocketbook on her arm. My mother held the phone up to her ear, no doubt calling me. My phone rang. I ignored it, because at that moment, she saw my truck. She moved the phone away from her head, and my phone stopped ringing.

I steered across the lot to a parking spot near them and parked the truck. Of course, they all stared.

"Hey, there's the racecar driver," Stevie said when I opened the door.

"That ticket's likely to cost you a good penny," my dad said.

"You really should slow down, dear," my grandmother said. "There's no need to rush through life."

She said that after they had made me feel as if I had to arrive at the hotel within seconds.

I climbed out from behind the steering wheel. "Well, I was speeding for a reason."

My mother held her hand up. "I know what you're going to say. You were speeding because you wanted to get here in a hurry so that I wouldn't be worried. It's all my fault."

"Actually, that's not the reason at all," I said.

My mother's perfectly plucked eyebrows knitted together. "Well, you should've wanted to get here in a hurry, because I was worried."

"Someone was chasing me." I rushed the words so that she'd stop talking.

My mother clutched her chest. "What? Was it the killer?"

"Did you make a customer mad?" Hank asked.

Stevie laughed.

"Who was chasing you, dear?" my grandmother asked in a calm voice.

My brothers had stepped closer, because they didn't want to miss a word. Even my dad had managed to amble over.

"So tell us who was following you," Stevie urged with a gesture of his hands. "Don't keep us in suspense."

"I'm not sure who it was. A woman in a dark car, I think. It may have been a reporter."

"This is awfully strange," my mother said. "See, this is why I worry about you."

"Nothing surprises me with Celeste," Hank said.

"Who's talking?" I said. "Besides, this was just a one-time thing."

My mother scoffed. "I beg to differ."

"Okay, a one-time thing this month. Everything will settle down soon. Nothing to worry about."

"Why are reporters following you?" my dad mumbled.

"I think they want the scoop on what happened at the estate. Pierce and Caleb said that I shouldn't talk to them," I said.

"I agree with Caleb and Pierce on this one," Stevie said. "Knowing Celeste, she would inadvertently confess to the crime when faced with any questioning."

"I would not confess. I had nothing to do with it." I placed my hands on my hips.

"We know that you didn't do it, but the way you stumble around your words," Stevie said.

I laughed. "That's the pot calling the kettle black."

"All right, no arguing, you two," my mother warned with a point of her index finger.

Movement caught our attention. We turned and gave each other a curious glance. Someone was hiding behind the bushes.

"Did you see that?" I whispered.

"We should go check it out," Hank said.

"No, boys, you should stay put," my mother said, holding up her hand, as if that would stop them.

Of course, they didn't listen.

"Be careful." Worry cracked my mother's voice. "You don't know what kind of weirdos are around. And anyone hiding in bushes is certainly a weirdo."

I didn't bother to tell her I'd been known to hide in a bush or two before. My brothers rushed over to the bushes, with the rest of us following closely behind. We eased closer as if something might jump out at us.

My brothers provided no warning as they ran toward the landscaping. With legs straight, backs arched, and arms wide, they jumped into the bush as if swan diving into a pool. Now they lay on top of the bush with no words, only a couple of groans. At that second, a dark-haired woman raced from a nearby shrub. She screamed as she headed toward a silver SUV.

"Get her," Grammy yelled.

My grandma took off in a sprint. I'd never seen her run like that before. She left us in her dust.

"Don't run that fast, Grammy," I yelled as I ran after her. "You might break a hip."

The woman jumped into the silver vehicle. A man was behind the wheel. He shoved it into reverse, squealing the tires as he raced out of the parking lot.

Now that my grandmother had stopped running, I caught up with her. "Are you all right, Grammy?" I asked.

"Well, I am fine, but that woman wouldn't have been okay if I'd gotten a hold of her. I would have given her a piece of my mind. What was she thinking? Was that the woman who followed you?"

"That was a different one. I think they must be re-porters," I said.

"Well, for heaven's sake, why are they following you? You're not J.Lo."

"No, Grammy, I am not J.Lo." I had no idea that my grandmother knew Jennifer Lopez.

"You don't need the paparazzi following you," she said.

"I guess they just want to get the scoop on the murder."

"They could ask you without sneaking around."

"But I'm not going to tell them anything. Caleb and Pierce said it was better to just say 'no comment'."

My mother and brothers had walked up. Dad was over in the landscaping, trying to straighten up the bush that my brothers had tackled.

"What was that all about?" my mother asked.

I explained to her that we thought it was a reporter.

"Well, she nearly scared me to death." My mother clutched her chest. "Now that the commotion is over, I suppose we can get some lunch."

I checked my watch. "We have to hurry, because I really need to finish a painting."

My mother motioned to my father, who was still trying to straighten up that bush.

"It's all right, Eddie, leave it alone. It'll grow back," my mother said.

He groaned at my mother's comment, but ultimately gave in and joined us. We squeezed into the Buick and headed out onto the road. Of course, I had my eye out for more reporters. But as my grandmother had said, I wasn't J.Lo, so surely this wouldn't be much of a scoop for them for long. I couldn't believe that they were that relentless. When they wanted something, obviously, they went after it. They wouldn't stop until they got the whole story.

"Where are we eating?" my mother asked.

"I want pizza," Hank said.

"I want Chinese," Stevie said.

"Well, I want a burger," Grammy said.

"Burgers it is," my mother said.

"Tell me where to go," my father mumbled.

CHAPTER 5

Travel Trailer Tip 5:
Be patient. Traveling with a trailer can be
stressful. You can't find a killer in a day.

I located the nearest diner by doing a quick search on my phone. The closest location would be the best option. The faster we finished this meal, the faster I could get back to work.

"Do you have any details about what happened?" my mother asked.

"Nothing yet," I said. "I suppose it's still way too early."

"I hope they arrest someone soon," Grammy said.

Her little gray head barely peeked up over the top of the front seat, where she sat between my father and mother.

"What were you doing back there, anyway?" Stevie asked. "We left you at the trailer."

"I lost my keys," I said.

"That sounds about right," he said. "You're always losing something."

"Well, I lost my mind years ago around you guys."

"Ha ha," he said.

"I just can't believe it happened. I feel so terrible about it. That poor woman," my mother said.

"I'm glad that Celeste didn't go in there at the wrong time and get caught up with the killer, too," Grammy said.

"You should've seen the way those people were running out of there," I said. "I thought I would be trampled. It was like the running of the bulls. Not one person stayed to help her."

"No one saw the murder occur?" my mother asked.

"I heard the tour group came into the room and saw her lying there."

"The least they could have done was render first aid," Grammy said.

"What if the killer had still been there when you went back in?" my mother asked.

"I doubt the killer wanted Celeste," Stevie said.

"Well, you never know," my mother said. "People are crazy. And killers aren't exactly the smartest people."

"What is that supposed to mean?" I asked.

"Oh, killers think they're smart, but in the end, they get caught. They're not so smart after all," Grammy said.

"No offense, but I think I want to change the subject," I said.

"Of course, dear, you're still upset over what happened."

"It's probably those creepy paintings you paint," my father said.

"What do you mean, 'creepy'?" I said.

"All the spooky images . . . you should stop doing that," he said.

"It's not as if I have any control over it," I said. "I just paint, and that's what shows up."

"Always knew you're a little creepy," Hank said.

I poked him in the side with my elbow.

"Ouch," he said.

"No fighting back there," my mother said.

It felt like I was eight years old all over again.

"I hope no other ghosts show up," my grandmother said.

"Have you painted anything spooky lately?" my mother asked.

"Nothing I've painted lately has anything spooky," I said.

"Well, good. Maybe it'll stop," my father said.

I wouldn't count on it, I thought, but I didn't tell him that. Besides, I kind of liked getting hidden messages. I didn't think it was all bad. I totally understood my family's concern, though. The images were crazy at times, but if they helped in the long run, I figured it was worth it. I really wanted to get back, because I had the urge to paint now, and it was hard to push that out of my head once it was there.

The sign for the Over Easy Diner came into view. A drawing of eggs, bacon, and toast decorated the signage. Thankful for small blessings, we reached the diner without further incident. Well, until we actually got into the parking lot. A silver SUV whizzed into the lot and into a parking space that we were getting ready to take. Oh boy. This probably wouldn't go well. I felt the tension ooze off my brothers.

"What's this jerk think he's up to?" Hank said.

A stocky, balding man got out of the SUV, flashed us an obscene hand gesture, and walked into the diner. Was that the same SUV we'd just seen?

"That certainly was rude," my mother said.

"Do you want us to move the car?" Stevie said.

Stevie and Hank put their hands on the car door handles, just waiting for the okay to make the move.

"No, don't do that. No lifting of the vehicle in the parking lot," I said. "There's another parking spot right over there. That will work just fine."

"But that isn't the original parking spot," Hank said.

"It's even better, because we will have a view of our car from inside the diner," I said.

I'd learned to be pretty good at defusing situations over the years. Now I just had to continue that once we got inside the restaurant. My brothers kept their eyes on that car as if it were the vehicle's fault. When we stepped into the diner, they shifted their focus onto the driver, who was at the counter talking to a tall, dark-haired waitress.

My grandmother grabbed my brothers by their arms. "Why don't you all help me to my seat."

She was pretty good at defusing situations, as well. I must have learned from her. The man didn't even notice us. I was sure he took people's parking spaces all the time. I was just glad that it seemed as if we'd moved on from the incident and could enjoy our food.

I was anxious to get back to the trailer and the painting. As soon as we sat down, I grabbed a napkin and pulled a pen from my purse. I wanted to start sketching an idea in my head before my mind went into overload.

Too many thoughts in my head would clutter it up, and I would feel like I was going to explode.

Every so often, I paused my sketching so that I could keep my eye on the parking-space thief. I had to make sure that my brothers didn't say anything else to him. After a few more minutes of talking to the waitress, the man turned and left. I assumed he hadn't even ordered food or anything. Thank goodness that was over. Now we just had to get to our meal, and then I could be back to my trailer. Curiosity got to me, though, and I wanted to see what the man was doing next.

"I'll be right back," I said, setting my pen down.

"Where are you going?" my mother asked.

"To the ladies' room." I smiled, hoping that they wouldn't see through my lie.

No doubt they would watch to see where I really went. The diner was small, and they would be able to keep track of me. I should have said I was going outside to the car. Oh well, it was too late now. My mother eyed me suspiciously, as I figured she would.

Without another word, I headed across the diner's floor. I kept my eye on the outside as I walked. The man was standing beside his car, but he hadn't gotten in yet. He was on his phone, moving his arms about as if in an argument with someone. It didn't surprise me at all to see him arguing. Not after the way he acted when we first encountered him in the parking lot.

What must it be like to constantly argue with people and have such negativity? What a nasty disposition. It was much more pleasant to go through life being nice to people and receiving kindness in return. I firmly believed in karma. People got back what they gave out. Maybe not all the time, but it didn't hurt to try positivity.

I'd almost made my way to the ladies' room now and probably wouldn't be able to see how this ended. Why was I interested in this man? Possibly because he seemed to be up to no good. I suppose it was my sixth sense peeking through. Once inside the ladies' room, I stared at my reflection in the mirror. Why didn't anyone tell me I had mascara smudged under my eye? I got a paper towel and wiped off the black mark. Next, I washed my hands. Was that enough time?

It would have to be enough, because I wanted to get back out there and see if the man was still in the parking lot. I hurried out the restroom door and focused my attention on the windows again. Unfortunately, he was gone. I felt a glimmer of relief, knowing no more confrontations were imminent.

Feeling the sensation of being watched, I noticed the waitress focusing on me. Had she noticed me paying attention to the man? He seemed quite a lot older than her. Was that her father? I smiled at her, but she remained expressionless. It was almost as if she gave me a glare. I hoped she wasn't our waitress.

"Is everything all right?" my mom asked when I sat back down.

"Of course; why wouldn't everything be all right?" I smiled.

"She's all right," Hank said. "She's always weird."

I tossed a napkin at him. He laughed.

I ordered a hamburger, just like Grammy, but I knew it wouldn't be as good as my Aunt Patsy's burgers. She had a special touch that I knew no one else could rival. My mother and Grammy were good cooks, too. I wished I had a slice of my mother's double chocolate cake. Or maybe a plate of Grammy's funnel cakes. When I had the time, I'd been known to whip up a delicious dish or two. I felt like my best recipes were the peanut butter cookies and the caramel-coconut brownies.

My family talked and laughed as we ate our lunch. As wacky as they were, I felt lucky to have them in my life. They were always there for me—in good times and bad. After finishing up the meal, we headed for the door. My father paid at the register. The waitress who had been eyeing me was the one who took the money. She barely acknowledged him, but she looked at me a couple of times.

"Should have let us move that car," Stevie said as we walked across the parking lot.

"Oh, for heaven's sake, let it go. We'll never see that man again," I said.

We squeezed back into the Buick. My father whizzed out of the space and pointed the car in the direction of the hotel. I'd gotten good at holding on while in the car with my dad. Every time we took a turn, it was like being on the Tilt-A-Whirl at the county fair. Fortunately, nothing else happened while we were at the diner or on the way back to the hotel. No strange cars followed us. Maybe that craziness was over. I'd successfully survived the lunch with my family and made it back to my trailer. It was time to paint. Would a mysterious image appear?

Homemade Funnel Cakes

Like doughnuts, but easier!
(Makes 8 cakes)
Prep time 15 minutes/Cook time 5 minutes

Ingredients
2 eggs
3 cups all-purpose flour
1 cup milk
½ teaspoon vanilla extract
¼ cup sugar
3 teaspoons baking powder
¼ teaspoon salt
Oil for frying
Powdered sugar

In a large bowl, beat eggs.

Add milk and vanilla until well blended.

In separate bowl, whisk flour, sugar, baking powder, and salt.

Beat dry ingredients into egg mixture until smooth.

Using a skillet, heat oil to 375 degrees.

Covering the bottom of a funnel with your finger, place half a cup of batter into the funnel.

Funnel batter in a spiral motion into skillet.

Fry until golden brown for two minutes on each side.

Drain and then dust with powdered sugar.

CHAPTER 6

Travel Trailer Tip 6:
Add a pop of color to the interior of your
travel trailer. It will help liven up the place
even more when the ghosts appear.

When the urge to paint came over me, I had to do it right away, before the inspiration faded. That was why I'd been in such a hurry to get back from lunch. A face popped up in my mind, and I knew I had to paint it, though I had no idea who this person was or even if he was real. Maybe this was just my imagination. Maybe it was much more than that.

Recently, I had painted portraits that had turned out to be spirits from the great beyond. Every time I painted an image of a person, I wondered if they would pop up out of thin air and start talking to me. It was spooky and exciting at the same time. In addition, the hidden images in my paintings usually conveyed some hidden message that I had to decipher.

There was a dazzling blue sky and perfect temperature

of seventy-two degrees, so I decided to paint outside. Fresh air was just what Van and I needed. After arriving back from the lunch with my family in one piece, I pulled out a blank canvas and retrieved my paints from the trailer. I set up my workstation in front of the trailer. The sun bathed the whole area in a warm yellow glow, and the tree branches swayed with the gentle breeze. Placing the canvas on the easel, I sat down in front of it, picking up the brush and dipping it into the burnt brown color.

"Let's see if we know this fellow, Van," I said.

Van sat at my feet, staring up at the canvas as if waiting to see what might magically appear. The man's face came first, because that was the most prominent part of the image that appeared in my mind. My excitement bubbled over as I waited to see my subject on the canvas and guess who he might be. I enhanced his bright blue eyes with specks of green and quickly filled in the rest of his features. With light strokes, I added streaks of auburn to his brown hair. I colored in his thin pinkish lips.

I stopped and studied the portrait. As far as I knew, I'd never met this man. This painting probably represented nothing more than my artistic mind at work. Maybe the paranormal experiences were over. Did I want that to be the case? Maybe I secretly enjoyed visits from the spirit world. I always said the ghosts scared me, but deep inside, I found them somewhat thrilling, too. Next, I added his clothing, just from the waist up, since that was all that I saw. He wore a suit that seemed like a style from the turn of the last century.

"I don't know this man, Van. Any guess on who he is?" I asked, pointing with the paintbrush.

Van covered his eyes with his paw.

"You're no help," I said.

Once I finished the painting, I set my brush down and studied the man's face. His eyes stared back at me as if he knew exactly what he was doing and what I was thinking.

"I still don't recognize him, Van," I said.

He barked, and his whole body lifted from the ground.

I blew the hair out of my eyes. "I suppose it's just my imagination and not a real person after all."

I'd almost forgotten to check the portrait for a hidden image. Lifting the jar that had held my paintbrushes up to my eye, I scanned the painting. I knew this must seem crazy to others, but it was the only way to see the hidden images. I had no idea why or how it worked, but I did it anyway. Going up and down, sideways, and all around, I saw nothing out of the ordinary.

"Nothing there, Van," I said.

He licked his paws as if unconcerned.

After cleaning up the supplies, I decided I'd move on with my pursuit of investigating this morning's horrific event. Pierce and Caleb would tell me not to get involved, obviously, but I wouldn't let that stop me. They'd see that this was for the best.

I changed Van's shirt to the black one with the word SECURITY on the back in white letters. We headed out toward the mansion. I would have to hurry, though, because I still had paintings to finish that I wanted to put out for sale. And to think that earlier I thought I was all set for the craft show. I'd only been kidding myself. I was always running behind, it seemed.

"We're going to get to the bottom of this, Van," I said as he marched along beside me.

I held his leash as we made our way over to the ticket-purchasing area. With any luck, I'd find someone willing to talk with me about today's events. I hoped people didn't realize that I'd been the one to discover the body. Technically, others had seen it first, but they'd run away. After reaching the front area of the mansion, Van decided he had to sniff the grass. I paused to give him a few seconds of fun time.

"What an adorable little dog," a dark-haired young woman said. She looked like a college student in her horn-rimmed glasses and holding a notebook.

Van wagged his tail, relishing the attention.

"Thank you," I said with pride.

"Is it all right if I pet him?" she asked.

I explained to her the process in order to pet Van. There were rules set up for her safety. Not because Van was a bad dog. Strangers scared Van when they tried to touch him. I totally understood why Van felt that way. All he saw was a giant person leaning down to attack him. That was his perspective, but once he knew that their intentions were good, he was fine. Belly rubs were one of his favorite things, along with treats, toys, and bones.

"Just hold your hand out and let him sniff it. And don't try to go behind his head, or he'll think you're attacking him," I said.

Her big dark eyes widened, as if maybe she were reconsidering. But ultimately, she did as I instructed, and everything was fine. Van had made a new friend. Even better, it appeared that she worked at the estate.

At least, that was what I assumed, considering she was wearing the same navy-blue uniform worn by the other tour guides. CHERYL was written on her name tag. I wondered if she was nervous, knowing that one of her colleagues had been murdered just hours earlier. Surely the answer to that was yes.

"You work at the estate?" I asked. "As a tour guide?"

"Yes," she said with a smile.

Apparently, she didn't know my identity.

"I'm here for the craft fair," I said.

"Oh, how nice," she said.

I wasn't sure how to approach the subject of the murder.

"Well, it's nice here, but after what happened earlier . . ." I said.

I hoped that she would take the bait.

She shook her head. "It was tragic. Ellen McDonald was a nice woman."

"Did you know her well?" I asked.

"No, I only recently started working here a few months ago. We spoke on and off. She seemed nice, though."

"Was there anything out of the ordinary that happened before her mishap today?" I asked, trying not to sound as if I were a private investigator.

"Well . . ." She surveyed around, as if she were checking to make sure no one was watching us.

I doubted anyone would think we were gossiping, but maybe they would.

"I know her friend was here this morning right before it happened. I didn't see her leave, but I did see her show up. Maybe she snuck out right after she killed her. They were arguing, or at least that's what I heard."

"What's her friend's name?" I asked.

It was important to get the details right away before she stopped talking. Maybe she'd realize what I was trying to do and clam up. The tour guide scowled. She probably wondered what difference it made and why did I want to know.

"Her name is Deidre Ashley," she said. "Why do you ask?"

"Oh." I chuckled. "I thought I might know her."

"Why would you know her? You're not from around here, are you?" Suspicion filled the woman's questions.

She was asking too many questions.

"No, actually, I'm not from around here," I said.

I had no explanation for why I'd thought I might know Deidre, so I just remained quiet. The guide was probably starting to think that I was a few nuts short of a fruitcake.

"Well, I hope they find who did this soon. I bet it will have an effect on attendance to the tours and the craft fair," she said.

Whew. Lucky for me, she'd changed the subject.

"I'm sure that management will want to keep it low-key, but the police will want to keep it in the news so that they can possibly get clues on who did it."

"Yes, I'm sure they will. Well, I need to go. It was nice talking to you." She patted Van again.

When she walked away, I picked up Van and headed to a nearby oak tree so that he could sniff around some more. "At least we got a few details, right, Van?" That's when I heard a whispered voice.

"Psst."

I checked over my shoulder to see if someone was trying to get my attention. No one was back there. It must've been my imagination. No sooner had I turned around than the noise came again. Okay, I was sure I heard it that time. It was definitely not my imagination, but no one was nearby. This was strange.

"Did you hear that, Van?" I asked.

He licked my cheek. That wasn't a direct answer. It was more like a can-we-go-for-a-treat-now response.

"Over here," a male voice said.

I spun around. That had definitely been someone talking, but I saw no one. Was someone playing tricks on me?

"Caleb, is that you?"

I wouldn't put it past him to try a trick like that. He was somewhat of a prankster, but this wasn't funny. After all, there had been a murder at the estate, so that meant I was a wee bit on edge. When Caleb didn't respond, I grew even more nervous. It didn't sound like my brothers' voices, either. However, maybe they were trying to disguise their voices so that they could play a trick on me, too.

I placed my hand on my hip. "Is that you, Stevie or Hank? If it's you guys, I'm gonna let you have it. No joking around."

"Over here," the male voice repeated.

I whirled around again, but still no one was in sight.

"I'm not playing this game anymore," I yelled out. "And I don't think it's funny."

"Over here," the voice said, even louder this time.

"Do you need help?" I asked. "Because if so, you need to tell me where 'over here' is. I can't see you."

"Over here," he said again, as if he were becoming agitated with me.

He wasn't the only one agitated. I stepped over to a nearby tree and anxiously peeked around the edge. There was no one hiding behind it.

"Well, if you can't tell me where 'over here' is or what you want, I'll just have to ignore you."

"Don't go," the male voice said.

This was really starting to creep me out. It sent shivers along my spine. Van barked and growled, as if he sensed or saw something that I didn't.

"Is someone hiding, Van?" I asked.

He growled while staring right at a nearby tree.

"Is someone behind that tree?" I asked.

It wasn't a large tree, so I wasn't sure how anyone could use its trunk to conceal their presence. Regardless, I walked over and peeked behind it. There was no one there.

"Okay, that's it, I'm done with this," I said in frustration. I would act as if I hadn't heard the person trying to get my attention. "Let's get out of here, Van. At least we have a name to start with, so something productive came of my conversation. We need to track down Deidre right away."

"Who's Deidre?" the male voice asked.

I spun and tumbled backward, landing on my bottom, when I realized the man from my portrait was standing right there. He wore the same dark, gray-striped suit as in the portrait. The jacket fit slightly loose, with wide lapels and a three-button closure. A matching vest peeked out from under his jacket, with a white dress shirt underneath. The thin, richly jewel-toned maroon tie finished his stylish outfit. Van barked and licked my face. That was his way of making sure I was all right. The man seemed just as real as any other person at the craft fair.

I was speechless. I should have been used to this, because it had happened in the past, but every time was just as shocking as the first. Even though I had somewhat expected a ghost to appear again at some point, I was never really prepared. He stared at me, waiting for an answer.

"Who are you?" I asked.

I couldn't answer his question about who Deidre was until I knew who *he* was. Why did he want to know, anyway? Did he have something to do with the murder? Perhaps he'd been in the estate at the time.

A deep line was entrenched between his eyebrows. "Well, oddly enough, my name has slipped from memory."

"Oh no. That's terrible," I said as I climbed up from the ground.

Was he being truthful or just trying to hide his identity? I suppose I would have to push for more details. Since I was still fairly new to all this paranormal stuff, I had to keep my guard up. I had no idea if I could trust a ghost to tell the truth.

"Was that you trying to catch my attention?" I asked.

"Yes, that was none other than me. I apologize. You see, I'm trying to figure out how this afterlife business works. I could see you, but you couldn't see me. Not at the moment, obviously. All of a sudden, poof . . ." He waved his arm. "Here I am, right before your eyes. You heard me before seeing me."

"Oh yes, I guess that was dramatic for you," I said.

"I'm just glad it worked out. I was beginning to panic," he said.

He was beginning to panic? I was pretty much always in a panic, wondering when a ghost would pop up. I had my answer . . . here was another one. Was he coming from another dimension, and it took a while to fully form into a person that I could see? And how long would he be here? Would he disappear in the next few minutes, or was he here permanently?

"For years I've been trying to get someone to see me. You came along and painted me. I was drawn to you because of that. I sensed that you could see me if I tried hard enough to come through."

"I don't know what to say," I said.

I waited until a few people walked by to continue talking, because I didn't want them to see me talking to my-self. I assumed they couldn't see the ghost. However, I had no way of knowing for sure unless I asked, and that wasn't happening. I could just see it now: me asking strangers if they saw the man I was talking to, and all they saw was a little dog at my feet.

My best friend, Samantha—or Sammie as everyone calls her—had seen the last ghost that came around, so I knew it was sometimes possible for others to see the ghosts. I suppose they had to have a trace of a sixth sense, as well. Sammie was open to that kind of thing, so it was no wonder that she saw the ghosts sometimes, too. Now that the group of people had walked away, I focused my attention on the ghost again. He was waving at Van as Van wagged his tail.

"Where did you come from?" I asked.

"From your painting, of course," he said. "That's all I know."

"Of course," I said with a click of my tongue.

Van ran in circles again and wagged his tail in excite-ment. I'd never seen him this happy to meet a stranger. This behavior was usually reserved for when he wanted a treat. I studied the man's face as he watched Van. He ap-peared just as he had in the painting, with a receding hair-line and a gray beard that was not in a current style. Instead of hair on the chin, there were large sideburns along the sides of his face. Could I get him to share any other details he might remember about his life? If he couldn't recall his name, he likely couldn't remember anything else. Nonetheless, I'd give it a shot and ask.

"Are you from the area?" I pressed.

I sounded as if I were talking to another tourist. This whole exchange was awkward. Too bad there wasn't a book on how to chitchat with a ghost. And not by a séance, but in a one-on-one conversation. Something that would help me with what questions to ask would be nice.

"Yes, I am attached to this estate," he said, puffing his chest out proudly.

"Interesting," I said.

Information like that should be something easy to re-search. Why was he attached to the estate? Had he lived here? Had he worked here? Now that I thought about it, a Vanderbilt had built this place. Yes, that was right . . . William Vanderbilt had built the mansion. Perhaps I should ask if that was his name.

"Is your name William Vanderbilt?" I asked.

He stared blankly at me, and suddenly, his eyes lit up. "Yes, that's it—William."

Wow. I was talking to a Vanderbilt. Sammie would never believe this. Well, actually, no one would believe this, and I wouldn't blame them, because it was crazy. No way would I tell my family about this. My brothers teased me enough already. No need to provide them with ammunition. I had a famous ghost coming through from the great beyond. Maybe I needed to paint Elvis Presley and see if he'd visit.

"Why are you here, Mr. Vanderbilt?" I asked.

"That I do not know," he said.

Another mystery for me to unravel. We stared at each other, unsure of what to say next. Would Mr. Vanderbilt hang around with me? How odd would that be?

"What is your name, young lady?" he asked.

Oh no. I'd forgotten that I hadn't introduced myself. How rude of me.

"My name is Celeste Cabot, and this is Van." I ges-tured.

Van circled again and wagged his tail.

"It's a pleasure to meet you both," Mr. Vanderbilt said with a smile.

"I was just taking Van for a walk," I said.

"You never answered my question," he said.

"What question is that?"

"Who is Deidre?"

"Oh, right. She's a friend of someone who was murdered here today." I watched his face for a reaction.

"Murdered here at the Biltmore Mansion?" he asked with shock in his voice.

"Yes, that's right," I said.

CHAPTER 7

Travel Trailer Tip 7:
Embrace the small space; don't fight it.
There's enough fighting with others. You
don't want to fight with yourself, too.

The sun shimmered across a shiny silver trailer as it pulled up to the arts and crafts fair. Another late arrival. Chirping birds perched on the branches of the nearby oak tree. It sounded as if they wanted to be a part of the conversation with the ghost, as well. A feather-soft breeze tickled my face. I still tried to wrap my mind around the fact that I was outside, talking to a spirit I'd painted.

"I had hoped you might be here to give me information about the murder," I said to the ghost. "Maybe you witnessed something inside the estate."

"Good heavens, no. I think I would remember seeing something so violent. Though I suppose my memory is a tad foggy, isn't it?" He tapped the side of his head with his index finger.

"Yes, just a smidgen," I said. "Maybe you'll recall."

He cast his gaze downward at his shiny black lace-up boots. "Perhaps. Who was murdered?"

"A woman who works here. I found her body," I said.

"How awful."

"Yes, it was."

"They don't know who did it?" he asked.

"No, but that's what I'd like to find out," I said.

"That sounds dangerous," he said.

I would have loved to stay in the great outdoors and chitchat with him, but I really needed to find the woman's friend. And I had no idea where to start with that.

"Well, I need to find this woman, Deidre Ashley," I said. "So I should be going."

"Wonderful," he said, clapping his hands together. "Where are we going?"

I had a feeling he would say that.

"I suppose I can check for her address," I said.

"That sounds like a daunting task," he said. "Wherever will you start?"

I pulled out my phone. "I'll Google it."

I typed in the woman's name.

"You'll what it?" he asked with confusion.

"I'll search online," I added.

"On what?" he asked.

"I know you're a ghost, but haven't you been snooping around and watching people? They hold these telephones in their hands. Like tiny computers on the go?"

"A computer?" His brow pinched together.

"I suppose you have no idea what I'm talking about."

"I've seen them holding those things up to their faces, but I had no idea what they were," Mr. Vanderbilt said.

"Well, I don't have time to go into much detail, but basically you can type in anything you want to know, and you'll get your answer." I held up the phone so that he could see.

"Amazing," he said.

"Yes, it is amazing," I said.

Naturally, I'd done my research before I'd come here for the craft fair. Based on my findings, I knew that the estate was the largest private residence and a national historic landmark.

"What about me? Can you find out anything about me on that contraption?" Mr. Vanderbilt asked.

"I suppose I could try."

I'd never anticipated needing to research Mr. Vanderbilt. Later, I'd discover that my research on him had been all wrong. I did a quick search on my phone as Mr. Vanderbilt watched in anticipation.

"What are you reading?" he asked.

"You opened the house on Christmas Eve, 1895."

"That sounds about right," he said.

I read down for further information. "You married June 1, 1890."

"Hmm, I don't remember that. Was she beautiful?"

"I'm sure of it," I said with a smile. "That was in Paris, France. None of this is coming back to you?"

"No, not really," he said.

"Oh," I said through pursed lips. "Well, let me read more and see if I can possibly spark more of your memories."

Mr. Vanderbilt paced. I figured he was anxious to hear what I discovered. If he didn't stop pacing, though, I might be too nervous to even continue.

"Your daughter was born on August 22, 1900."

"Okay," he said.

"None of this is clicking with you?"

"No, not really," he said.

"She was married in April 1924."

"No," he said.

"Okay, you were involved in overseeing the care of the Biltmore house."

"Well, that would make sense, considering I owned the home," he said.

"Yes, I suppose it would, wouldn't it? Maybe this information will come back to you soon. Once it has time to settle in your mind."

"That's probably what will happen," he said with a forced smile.

"Don't worry. I'll just enjoy your company."

Not that I cared having Mr. Vanderbilt around, but it was distracting having a ghost following me. Nevertheless, I wanted to help him if there were some reasons why he was still hanging around. Maybe I could figure that out, and he could move on to the next dimension.

"Did you find out what you need to know about the woman?" he asked.

"As a matter of fact, I found an address. I don't know if it's correct, but it's some place to start." I pointed at my phone.

"It can't hurt to try, can it?" he asked.

"I won't even answer that question, because I've had bad luck in the past with wrong decisions. Just when I think something is a good idea, it turns out to be the opposite."

"That's a shame," he said with a click of his tongue.

"We'll drive over in my truck," I said.

I knew he wouldn't let me go alone. Mr. Vanderbilt followed me as I carried Van toward my pink F-1. Yellow and red flowers lined the stone path that led to the parking lot. Trees on either side swayed with the warm, gentle breeze.

"Do you take the dog with you everywhere?" he asked.

"Not everywhere. Sometimes he gets tired and likes to take naps. If some place is dangerous, I won't take him."

"What if the place today is dangerous?"

"If I think it is dangerous, I'm not going anywhere near it. We'll find out when we get there."

"I don't like the sound of that," he said.

Soon, we reached my truck. The sun bounced off the shiny chrome, and the pink color stood out like a puff of cotton candy.

"It's pink," Mr. Vanderbilt said.

"Yes, it is pink," I said with a smile. "I love pink."

"I've seen these things before, but I've never been in one," he said.

"Well, I guess this will be your first time." I opened the driver's side truck door and motioned for him to get in.

He tried to open the door just like me, but his hand went right through the truck's door.

"I think you could just move right through it without opening the door," I said. "But I'm no paranormal expert."

He made a running lunge for the truck and slipped right in. What would happen, though? Would he be able to sit in the truck? It sure seemed as if it would work out that way.

"That was a pretty cool trick," I said.

"Thanks for the tip," he said, giving me a thumbs-up.

He sat there just like any living human. When I first saw a ghost do this, I figured they would just fall right through the seat, like when Mr. Vanderbilt tried to open the door. Once again, though, I didn't understand all the paranormal stuff and how it worked. After I slipped behind the wheel, Van sat next to me. He had love in his eyes for Mr. Vanderbilt. I'd never seen Van make a friend so quickly. I turned the truck's ignition and shifted it into gear.

"I hope this is a successful visit," Mr. Vanderbilt said as he took in the scenery.

"Me too." With the truck in reverse, I tapped the gas and backed out of the spot.

Soon, we were on the road and headed to our destination. Within seconds, I noticed a black car following me. It was the same one that had gotten me the speeding ticket. No way! I wasn't going to let the driver get by with it this time, although I had no idea what I would do to stop her. I didn't want to talk to her about the murder, but I didn't want her following me, either.

"I can't believe she's following me again," I said.

After noticing me checking the rearview mirror, Mr. Vanderbilt peered over his shoulder. "Who is following you?"

"A reporter. She wants to know more about the murder. But I'm not talking to her!"

"Just ignore her," he said in a raised voice.

"I would ignore her, but I don't want her to know what I'm up to and where I'm headed. She should just leave me alone. I only found the dead woman. I had nothing to do with the murder."

"Of course not," Mr. Vanderbilt said.

He said that, but did he really believe me? The tone of his voice didn't sound completely confident.

I scanned the area to see if there was any way I could lose her. "Can you believe they think I might have done something like that?"

"Well, you don't seem like a murderer to me," he said.

Whew. Maybe he believed me, after all.

"Thank you, Mr. Vanderbilt," I said with a smile. "It's encouraging to get a compliment reassuring me that I don't seem like a murderer."

What had I gotten myself into? Most times, I'd be happy with compliments telling me that my hair looked nice or that the person liked my dress. Not that I didn't appear as if I had strangled someone.

The woman following me was wasting precious time. It would take even longer for me to reach my destination, because I'd have to spend my time getting rid of her. One important thing, though: I had to remember, no speeding this time. I couldn't afford another ticket. Actually, I couldn't afford the one I'd gotten, much less another.

The traffic light up ahead remained green. It had been that way for quite some time, I thought. Maybe if it turned yellow, I could scoot through, and then it would turn red and catch her. With any luck, if that happened, I would lose her. At least, that was the way it played out in my mind. Reality might have a different plan for me.

I drove closer to the light. "Come on, turn yellow."

A couple of seconds later, the signal did just as I asked.

"Oh, I'm excited. Here's my chance," I said.

I slowed down to make sure that the woman wouldn't have a chance to drive through the yellow light, as well. I hoped she didn't try to run a red light. That could be extremely dangerous. Surely, she wasn't that crazy. This was risky business. After making my way through the yellow light, I saw that she had to stop.

"Yes, it worked," I said with excitement.

"Good work," Mr. Vanderbilt said. "Your driving skills are quite impressive."

I sped up in order to get away before she caught up. However, I couldn't speed too much, because I had that fear of receiving another ticket looming over me. Every few seconds, I glanced in the mirror. So far, there was no sign of the black car. Would that silver SUV pop up next?

"I think I lost her," I said.

"You certainly outsmarted her," he said.

"More like I just got lucky, but I'll take it."

At least I was able to relax a smidgen. I remained on edge, though, because I had no idea when she'd return. Even without the car following me, I had a nervous stomach about finding Deidre. I tapped my fingers against the steering wheel with anxious energy.

"You're making me nervous," Mr. Vanderbilt said.

"Sorry," I said. "Nervous habit, I suppose."

"No reason to be nervous. She's not behind you."

"I'm worried about finding Deidre. Plus, the woman in the black car might show up again. Not to mention that other silver vehicle I saw earlier. Reporters were actually hiding in the bushes."

"Well, you shouldn't worry about the things you can't control. We'll change the subject. Why don't you tell me more about yourself?" Mr. Vanderbilt said.

"What would you like to know?" I asked.

"Are you from around these parts? I fell in love with this area, although I'm not originally from here."

"Yes, I know, I read about you, remember? Oh, you remembered something about yourself," I said excitedly.

"Yes, I suppose I did," he said around a chuckle.

"I'm not from here, either, but I live close by. I just came for the craft fair. I'm an artist," I said with a smile. "What else would you like to know about me?"

"How did you come about this talent of painting spirits?"

"I'm not sure," I said. "Maybe I should try to figure that out someday, but I don't know. I suppose there are questions that we can never answer."

"It's certainly a strange talent," he said. "I would want to know if I were you."

He didn't know the half of my strange talents. The worst part was the mystery images that I painted. They spooked me way more than the actual spirits. Soon, we pulled up to the street address that I'd found for Deidre Ashley. I turned left onto Adams Street.

"Are you sure this is the location?" Mr. Vanderbilt asked.

"I'm not positive, but it's definitely a start. I have to do something to find her," I said.

I counted down the house numbers. The white one on the left had the numbers written on the mailbox by the curb. Just as I was approaching the home, a car was backing out of the driveway. I eased off the gas.

"Maybe that's her," I said.

"Well, you should follow her," Mr. Vanderbilt said.

"I'll give it a try," I said.

My adrenaline was really pumping. Again, I was in my pink truck, which was kind of like a neon sign traveling down the road. If I wanted to search for a murderer, maybe I needed to get a car that wasn't so obvious. Nevertheless, it was all I had at this time. Besides, I loved my truck. And I definitely wouldn't get rid of it.

"Can you tell who's behind the wheel?" he asked.

"No, maybe I can if I get closer." I pushed the gas pedal. "Luckily, the driver doesn't know who I am, so she won't think that I'm following her."

"If this person thinks you're following them, you could be putting yourself in great danger," Mr. Vanderbilt warned.

"I won't let it get that far out of hand," I said.

I pushed on the gas again so that I could catch up to the little black car.

"Why is her vehicle so small and yours so big?" he asked.

"It's called a smart car," I said.

"What is smart about it?" he asked. "Is yours dumb?"

I laughed. "Good question. I'm not sure. All I know is that it's tiny. I think it might be fuel-efficient."

"Oh," he said.

The driver took the next left and drove down a street that led out onto the main road. So far, I'd been successful with keeping up with her. I just hoped that it stayed that way. With more traffic, it might be more difficult to keep up. Wherever she was headed, I hoped that I got a chance to speak with her. Though I wasn't sure what I would say.

She turned on her signal, indicating that she would be making a right turn soon. At least she gave me advance notice. Maybe that meant she didn't realize I was actually following her. She turned into the parking lot of a large brick building. The parking lot was almost empty, and I wasn't sure that I should follow her there. I eased up on the gas and merged over onto the side of the road so that I could watch her movements.

There was no indication of what might be inside. Was the building not in use? Based on the length of the structure, I thought perhaps it had been a school.

"What do we do?" Mr. Vanderbilt asked.

"We'll watch and see what she does," I said.

CHAPTER 8

Travel Trailer Tip 8:
Remind yourself to observe your
surroundings. Traveling is all about seeing.
You'll see stuff you never noticed before.

The woman parked the car and after a few seconds got out, tossing her big black purse over her shoulder. With her slim figure and long legs, she gracefully headed toward the side door. The breeze blew waves of auburn-colored hair from her shoulders.

When she reached the door, it opened, and a stocky, bald-headed man let her inside. She stepped through the entrance, but he stayed there for a couple of seconds. Something nagged at the back of my mind. What was it?

He scanned the area as if checking to see if anyone was watching or following her. I ducked down in my seat just in case he happened to glance my way. Was he suspicious that someone was spying on him? He seemed paranoid. He wasn't doing a very good job of guarding, though, since he didn't realize I was watching. Good thing he didn't see the ghost, because Mr. Vanderbilt didn't duck down. The man stepped back inside, closing the door behind him.

Seconds later, the realization hit me. I recognized the man. He was the one I'd seen at the diner with my family. The one who had taken the parking space. He'd been rude at the diner, and he seemed mean this time, too. Apparently, he was consistent. Thank heavens he hadn't seen me. Would he recognize me, though? Probably not. He was probably rude to so many people that he lost track.

"I really want to know what's going on inside that building," I said.

"I don't see how that's possible," Mr. Vanderbilt said. "Again, why are you seeking this woman?"

"She had an argument with the woman who was murdered, and maybe she's the killer."

"You certainly don't want to go in there and confront her if she's a killer," he said.

"No, I certainly don't want that," I said as I opened the truck door.

"Where are you going?" Mr. Vanderbilt called out.

With Van in my arms, I walked around the front of the truck as Mr. Vanderbilt slipped out.

He met me at the right fender. "I thought you said you weren't going in there. Plus, you have the dog with you."

I shook my head. "No, I didn't say that I wasn't going in. I just said that I didn't *want* to go in, but this isn't a matter of *wanting* to go in, it's a matter of *having* to go in."

"I disagree with that," he said. "You don't have to go in there. Just let the police figure this out."

"That would be the wise thing to do, wouldn't it," I said.

"Absolutely. We'll go back to the mansion." He gestured toward the truck.

"I'm sorry, Mr. Vanderbilt, I have to go find out what they're doing. That doesn't mean I'll go in. I'll just take a little peek in one of the windows."

"You'd better hope that they don't catch you," he said.

"Oh, believe me, I hope they don't catch me." I held Van in my arms, and I certainly didn't want to put him in danger.

Mr. Vanderbilt followed me as I walked toward the building. The last thing I needed was for the man and woman to see me lurking around the property. The building had quite a few windows, and I couldn't see inside until I got closer. At that point, it might be too late. Of course, they didn't know who I was, right? If they caught me, I would just pretend like I was lost. They wouldn't kill me for that; at least, I hoped not.

Once I neared the building, I had to decide which window to peek in first. I supposed the one closest to the side door would be the best option. However, there were many to pick from. Windows lined the entire back of the building, and I suspected my early thought that it had once been an elementary school was correct. I spotted a couple of old swings and a jungle gym in the distance, nearly concealed by weeds and tall grass. Sun beat against the glass, and I worried that there might be too much glare for me to see in. I'd have to try, though, because in my opinion, this seemed extremely important.

Never mind that it might be hard to maneuver up to the windows because of all the overgrown landscaping. The bushes were acting as an obstacle course.

"Make sure not to fall and hurt yourself," Mr. Vanderbilt warned.

"I'll give it my best shot," I said.

I stepped closer to the building until I was right up next to the window. As I leaned forward, my face was almost touching the glass.

"What do you see?" Mr. Vanderbilt asked.

"So far, nothing," I said. "Oh, wait, here they come."

I ducked down so that they couldn't see me. My pulse raced at the thought of being caught.

"How will you know what they're doing if you don't check in the window?" he asked.

"I just want to make sure they don't see me." I inched back up to the window.

"What do you see?" Mr. Vanderbilt had moved to my side.

"The man and woman are standing in the room. They're talking. By some fortunate twist of fate, they haven't noticed me yet."

"You still can't find out what they are talking about," he said.

Mr. Vanderbilt was right about that. What would I do? The longer I watched them, the more chance I had of being discovered.

"Wait a minute." I turned to Mr. Vanderbilt. "They can't see you. Why am I sneaking around when you can just go in and watch them?"

He studied my face. "I can do that, sure, but we both know that you won't be satisfied. You'll want to see this for yourself."

After a pause, I said, "Yeah, you're right about that."

Turning back to the window, I peered across the room and noticed that the window on the other side was slightly ajar. Perhaps I could go over to the other side and hear what they were saying. It was at least worth a shot.

With anxiety in my stomach, I slipped down from the window and headed around the building.

"Where are you going?" Mr. Vanderbilt asked.

"I'm going to the other side to that window. It's open a little, and I hope I can hear what they're saying."

"Oh, just don't get caught," he said as he trailed along behind me. "You certainly like to live dangerously."

I didn't like living dangerously, but I felt this was necessary. Actually, I was quite scared. My panting and quickened pulse increased with each step.

Van was being good as I held him in my arms. Soon, he would become restless and want to get down to play, or he would be ready for food. With any luck the man and woman inside wouldn't stay too long. I hoped they didn't come out the side door as I was walking around. Of course, I would go with my plan and tell them that I was lost. Or better yet, I could pretend that I'd been searching for my dog. That would be perfect. Whew. At least I had a believable reason for traipsing around this building.

With great relief, I made it to the other side of the building without being detected. I hurried over to the window. On the count of three, I would make my move. I wasn't sure why I needed to count to three. I suppose to give myself time to mentally prepare. Or it was just more stalling.

I eased over and saw that the couple hadn't spotted me. They stood in the same location. There was no need for me to stare at them, though, so I took my position by the window and just listened.

"You said you would get me the item," the man said in a rough voice. "This is what we planned."

"I told you I would, and I will," the woman said.

"I've given you plenty of chances, Deidre. I'm not going to wait much longer."

The man was threatening her. What did he want from her? At least I knew that I was following the correct person.

"I just need a couple more days," she said.

A long silence filled the room, and I wondered what he would do next. I peeked in to see in the window. They were still in the same position, as if in a standoff. I hunkered down again before one of them caught me.

"Two more days."

"He held up two fingers," Mr. Vanderbilt recounted as he peered in the window.

"You'll meet me back here?" the man asked. "I assume at the same time and no longer than two days?"

"I promise I'll be here in two days," she said.

Two days? What was she trying to get in the next two days? Did this have anything to do with her friend's murder?

"I have to go," Deidre said.

There was no response from the man.

"Let go of me," she yelled.

CHAPTER 9

Travel Trailer Tip 9:
Don't block the windows in case you need to
see out . . . or in.

Jumping into action, I peeked through the window. Did I need to go in there and rescue her? What would I do to help? That man appeared awfully strong. Not to mention mean.

"This is extremely unsettling," Mr. Vanderbilt said.

"Yes, it is," I said.

Deidre yanked her arm from the man and rushed toward the side door. As luck would have it, he didn't go after her. I wasn't sure what I would have done to save her. Deidre was no bigger than me. We'd be like two mice trying to fight a bear.

"Aren't you going to follow her?" Mr. Vanderbilt asked.

"I don't think I will. It might be better to find out who that man is. She said it would be a couple days until she got the item, so I assume she isn't getting it now. It might be better to follow him."

"That sounds even more dangerous," he said. "You confuse me, Celeste Cabot."

"That's okay, Mr. Vanderbilt. I confuse myself, too," I said.

The man turned and headed in the opposite direction. I would have to actually enter the building. If Mr. Vanderbilt thought what I was currently doing was dangerous, then he really wouldn't like my next move.

"I have to catch up with him," I said.

"Oh no, don't do that," Mr. Vanderbilt said as he ran behind me.

"I have to," I said over my shoulder.

With all the other windows on the outside of the building, perhaps I could peek in one of those before actually trying to get in. The more I thought about that, the more anxiety settled in my stomach. What was I thinking? I couldn't just walk into the building. I would have to make up some kind of excuse and get in. Was there a main door to enter, or maybe a bell to ring for someone's attention? What was this place, anyway?

Shoving my way through the shrubbery, I hurried down to the next window. This one gave a view into a different room. The man stood by a desk, studying a sheet of paper in his hands. He had no idea I watched him. I tried to steady my breathing so that I wouldn't pass out from nervousness. Detectives didn't pass out on the job.

"What will you do, Celeste?" Mr. Vanderbilt asked.

That was a question I didn't have an answer for just yet. Unfortunately, I wouldn't have time to think of an answer. The man turned around, and our eyes met. My stomach dropped instantly, and panic spiked through my body. Even my toes tingled.

A scowl appeared on his face, and he yelled, "Who are you?"

He ran toward the window as if he might just jump right out at me. No way would I answer him.

"Run," I screamed to Mr. Vanderbilt.

Why had I screamed at Mr. Vanderbilt? It wasn't as if the man could see him. At least, I didn't think he saw him. I took off around the side of the building, hoping that I would make it to my truck before this man made it out the back door. Unfortunately, when I turned the corner, he burst out the door like a caged animal released. I was trapped.

After screaming rather loudly, I froze on the spot. My heart thumped wildly in my chest. The man ran over to me and grabbed me by the arms, much tighter than necessary.

"Take your hands off her," Mr. Vanderbilt yelled.

"Who are you and why are you spying on me?" the man demanded.

This was the perfect time to use that story I had concocted.

"I was just searching for my dog." I said in a shaky voice.

Van huddled close to my chest. He wouldn't even look at the stranger and shook just like me.

"What?" the man snapped.

"My dog took off, and I followed him here. I just happened to catch movement in the building. I wasn't trying to break in or watch you, I promise."

His dark, beady eyes remained focused on me. A jagged scar snaked across his right cheek. After what seemed like an eternity, he released his hold. I exhaled and tried to calm my nerves, although I wasn't convinced this was over. At any time, he could reach out and try to strangle me.

"This is private property," he said.

"You tell him that you're going to call the police for assaulting you," Mr. Vanderbilt said.

Maybe I'd better leave well enough alone and not mention that. I just wanted to get out of here as quickly as possible.

"You have your dog, so get out of here and don't come back," the man said.

I wished there were something I could do to find out who this man was and why Deidre had been here. But as angry as he was, I wasn't sure there was any way to bring up the subject.

"You should walk away," Mr. Vanderbilt said.

He had a good idea. Why was I still standing here, allowing this man to glare at me? Maybe it was because I wanted to ask more questions. Actually, not only did I want to ask more questions, I needed to ask. It was something out of my control. My anxiety was through the roof. I had to get up enough nerve. What was the worst that could happen? Okay, I wouldn't even think about the worst that could happen. Because that could be bad.

"By the way, what is this building?" I asked.

"Oh, dear. This isn't a good idea," Mr. Vanderbilt said. "He's even madder, and I wasn't sure that was even possible."

"I don't think that's any of your business," the man said.

I could find out on my own. I didn't need him. Though it would be much easier and faster if he'd just tell me. I supposed asking for his name would be out of the question, too.

"You really should leave," Mr. Vanderbilt urged.

I moved around the man and hurried toward the parking lot. I wished he wouldn't see what vehicle I got into, because once he saw it, he would never forget.

"Is he watching me?" I asked.

"Yes, his beady little eyes are burning a hole through you," Mr. Vanderbilt said.

That made me feel even worse. If my family were here, they'd surely let him have it. If Grammy had seen him put his hands on me, she would've smacked him with her pocketbook. And he certainly would have deserved it. I just wanted to get out of there.

"I've had an encounter with that man before," I said.

"Twice?" Mr. Vanderbilt asked. "That's unfortunate."

"He wasn't nice that time, either."

"That doesn't surprise me," he said.

"He took our parking space at the diner. My brothers were really angry. I won't bother to tell them that I ran into him again. The last thing I need is for them to come over here and confront this guy."

"He seems kind of unhinged. I'm concerned for Deidre."

"You're probably right. I'm really concerned, too," I said. "But what will I do about it?"

"That I don't know," he said. "Possibly you should contact the police."

"Yes, I suppose that would be the right thing to do."

Telling them that I was snooping around wouldn't be fun. I could use the same story about chasing after Van. Yeah, that probably wouldn't work with the cops.

"I hope you avoid any contact with this man in the future," Mr. Vanderbilt said.

"I can't guarantee that," I answered. "After all, Deidre is supposed to meet him in two days."

"I don't like the sound of this," Mr. Vanderbilt added.

"Sometimes things just have to be done. There are a lot of things I don't like. I would much prefer not to be involved in all of this and just do my craft fair. But I was sucked in." I tossed my hands up. "It was as if the universe was telling me I needed to solve this case."

"But why?" Mr. Vanderbilt asked.

"I hope to find out," I said.

Once at the parking lot, I turned toward the street.

"Where are you going?" Mr. Vanderbilt asked as he hurried beside me.

"I want to walk past so he won't see me get into the truck. I can wait until he's gone and come back for it."

"Oh, good thinking," he said.

As I headed down the sidewalk, I walked by the truck as if I'd never seen it before. How would I check to see if the man watched me? Take steady breaths, I reminded myself. Remain calm, I thought.

Once I was down the sidewalk, I hid behind a magnolia tree with Van in my arms. The scent from the large white flowers permeated the air. Van sniffed the air around him.

"This will seem awfully suspicious if anyone sees you," Mr. Vanderbilt said.

"The key is that no one will see me."

"That would be ideal, yes," he said. "Things don't always work out according to plans."

"You're telling me. Do you think he's gone?" I asked.

"I wouldn't see why not, unless he comes after you," Mr. Vanderbilt said.

"Oh, don't say that."

"Well, you have to think about the reality. He did seem angry."

"Yes, I suppose he was angry. I'll just take a peek out and see if he's there," I said.

"Don't worry, he's gone," Mr. Vanderbilt announced.

Was that true? I had to see for myself.

After counting to three to steady my anxiety, I peered out from around the tree. Thank goodness there was no sign of him, although he might still be beside the building, waiting for me to come back to the truck. Did he know it was mine? I couldn't wait here forever. I wanted to get out of there.

When a dog barked and growled right behind me, I jumped and spun around. A petite gray-haired woman stood behind me, holding a white-and-cream French Bulldog by a leash. It was good that he was restrained, because based on the display of his sharp white teeth, I assumed he wanted to take a bite out of my leg.

"What are you doing back there?" she asked suspiciously.

I didn't have a good answer for her question. It wasn't as if I could tell her I was playing hide-and-seek. Or could I?

"I'm hiding from someone," I said.

Her face scrunched up. "Do I need to call the police?"

"No, no." I gestured for her to stop.

This movement made the dog bark even louder, which would inevitably draw attention to us. Van yapped, too, as if the dogs were arguing with each other. The purpose of hiding behind the tree was to hide from the man, but if he checked this way to see why the dog was barking, he would spot me.

"Nice doggie," I said.

Of course, that made him bark more.

"You should get out of here," Mr. Vanderbilt said.

"The truth is, I have a stalker," I said. "And I thought I saw him."

"Oh no," Mr. Vanderbilt groaned.

"Well, you can never be too safe. You should report this to the police," the woman said.

"Oh, they know," I said. "But there's really nothing they can do. I just have to be careful."

"What a tangled web we weave," Mr. Vanderbilt said.

This little lie was just to get me out of the situation. It could be life or death.

The woman peered around. "I don't see anyone."

"I guess he's gone," I said, attempting a smile.

"What does he look like?" One of her bushy eyebrows wiggled upward like a caterpillar crawling on her forehead.

"Don't describe the man you just had an encounter with, or she'll probably go after him. She seems quite concerned."

Yes, I thought I'd scared the lady. That wasn't my intention.

"He's tall and wears eyeglasses. And he has a limp," I blurted out.

"Okay, you can stop," Mr. Vanderbilt said.

I supposed that was enough description.

"I think I would remember seeing someone who had a limp walking around here," she said.

"Yes, I suppose you would. I guess he's gone. Well, I should be leaving."

She stared at me for a little longer. The bulldog was getting antsy, and so was Van. She took a few steps. Luckily, she was leaving.

"Just be safe around here," she said.

"I most definitely will," I said.

"I'm glad she's gone," Mr. Vanderbilt said after the woman walked away. "My nerves are a mess."

"Your nerves? How do you think I feel?"

"Well, you kind of got yourself into the situation."

"I'm trying to solve a murder," I said. "I suppose I'll have to take a chance and go back to the truck."

"You'll probably never see the man again," Mr. Vanderbilt said, trying to make me feel better.

"That's not true," I said. "I have to find out why Deidre's meeting him and what the item is that he wants."

"Do you think it has something to do with the murder?"

"Maybe or maybe not, but I have to be sure. What if it does? This could be the clue to solving the case."

"I still say you should leave the detectives to do this."

"Well, not that I don't appreciate your input, Mr. Vanderbilt, but I have to disagree," I said.

I hurried out from behind the tree and down the sidewalk toward the truck. I was glad to see that the man wasn't waiting by the truck for me. As I got closer, I glanced over at the building. Whew. The man wasn't there. At least I could breathe easier. I quickened my steps and headed for the driver's door.

"You dodged a bullet," Mr. Vanderbilt said. "Figuratively, of course."

"Let's hope it stays that way," I said.

CHAPTER 10

Travel Trailer Tip 10:
If you can't get rid of guests, then enjoy
the closeness.

I'd just made it back to the estate when my phone rang. Mr. Vanderbilt scowled, trying to locate the source of the ringing.

"Celeste, I'm on my way. This will be fun," Sammie said when I answered.

My best friend Samantha Sutton was heading toward North Carolina to help me out at the craft fair. Mostly, she just wanted to tour the mansion. I had to tell her the horrible news.

"You're not going to believe this," I said.

"Oh, don't tell me they canceled the craft fair. I was as excited as a pig rolling in mud," she said.

"The craft fair is still on, as far as I know. However, I discovered a dead body."

It sounded even crazier when I said it out loud. A silence filled the connection.

"Are you still there?" I asked.

She chuckled nervously. "You're just kidding, right? You almost got me for a minute."

"I wish I was joking. Unfortunately, it's all too real."

"What happened?" Sammie asked.

I explained the whole sequence of events. Peeking out the window, I checked to make sure no reporters were lurking around.

"The craft fair is still going on as normal, though," I said.

"Maybe it's best to keep a hint of normalcy," Sammie said.

"I suppose," I said with hesitation in my voice.

"Did something else happen?" she asked.

"There's another ghost," I said.

Mr. Vanderbilt was playing with Van. He ran in a circle around the tiny kitchen area while Van chased him.

"Who is the ghost?" Sammie asked.

"Okay . . . here goes. I believe the ghost is William Vanderbilt."

Another pause. Mr. Vanderbilt heard his name and waved, as if Sammie could see his reaction.

"You mean the Vanderbilt who built the mansion?" Sammie asked in shock.

"Yes, that's the one," I said.

"How did that happen? Did you paint him?"

"Apparently, I did. Of course, not on purpose."

"Where is he? Is he with you?" Sammie asked. "I have to come. Do you think I'll see him, too?"

"It's possible. He's right here in the trailer with me, playing with Van. He's nice," I said.

"Well, I guess I should be on my way," Sammie said. "I don't want to miss him."

Mr. Vanderbilt had sat down on the sofa bench, and Van was trying to sit on the ghost's lap.

"I don't think you have to worry about missing him. It doesn't seem as if he's going anywhere anytime soon. Plus, I think he stays at the mansion all the time."

"Did he say why he's at the mansion, or why he came to you in a painting?"

"Not yet. Unfortunately, his memory is spotty. I hope he'll clue me in soon," I said.

"I hope so, too," Sammie said. "I'll see you in two shakes."

When I ended the call, I stood back from Mr. Vanderbilt's portrait and studied the work. Was there a hidden image in this painting that I had missed? Lately, not only had I painted ghosts, but I also painted strange hidden images within my paintings. I had no idea I was even doing it. Only after the fact did I see them, and only while peering at the art through glass.

This talent of mine had been stumbled upon by accident. It continued to happen, and I had yet to figure out why. Maybe I would never know the cause. Still, the hidden images had helped me solve a couple of mysteries. Was that the reason for Mr. Vanderbilt's appearance? Would new images help solve the Biltmore mystery?

"Why are you studying the painting for so long? Are you thinking about how handsome I am?" Mr. Vanderbilt asked with a laugh.

I chuckled. "Well, you are dashing, of course. But I'm searching for hidden images within the painting."

"What do you mean?" he asked.

"When I paint something, I've discovered that there are sometimes hidden things in the painting that I don't know I painted." I picked up the jar that I used for my brushes.

Squinting one eye, I peered through the glass at the portrait.

"That's a funny way of seeing it," he said.

"That's the way they appear," I said as I scanned the canvas.

"Do you see anything?" he asked.

Van's barking pierced the quiet little trailer, breaking my concentration. He wouldn't stop barking. Something was definitely wrong. I scooped Van into my arms and hurried over to the door to peek out the tiny window. I moved the curtain back just a smidgen. No one was there.

"What's happening?" Mr. Vanderbilt asked.

"I'm not sure," I whispered. "If Van barks like that, it means something is around. As far as I can tell, no one is here. It could be another animal."

"Maybe it's a person, and they're hiding," he said.

"Way to make me feel better, Mr. Vanderbilt. That's what I'm afraid of," I said.

I stood there for a few seconds longer, just in case I spotted someone.

"Maybe you're just spooked after what happened," Mr. Vanderbilt said.

"I guess that's possible."

Mr. Vanderbilt gestured toward the canvas. "Go back to the painting and tell me what you see. You've piqued my interest."

No sooner had I stepped toward the painting than a knock sounded against the door. I jumped, and my heart sped up. I knew that someone had really been around the trailer. Bless my tiny guard dog. I rushed over to the door.

"Don't open the door without checking out the window," Mr. Vanderbilt said.

"Don't worry, I won't," I said as I reached the door.

My anxiety was high as I inched the curtain back for a peek outside. No one was standing there.

"Who is it?" Mr. Vanderbilt asked.

"No one is out there," I said.

"That's impossible," he said. "They just knocked. Are you sure no one is there?"

"Maybe they took off quickly. Someone could be playing a trick on me."

"I can go out there and check," he said.

"That's a good idea," I said.

In a split second, Mr. Vanderbilt disappeared. Van and I waited with bated breath. I paced for a moment and went back to the door. This time, I didn't even see Mr. Vanderbilt.

"Where did he go, Van?" I asked.

"I'm right here, Celeste," Mr. Vanderbilt said from over my shoulder.

I spun around. "Oh, you scared me."

"Sorry about that," he said.

"What did you see?" I asked.

"I saw a man running after a dog."

Another knock sounded against the door. Van barked again. I knew his bark wasn't to alert me to a stranger. He was barking because he wanted to see Gum Shoe.

"Oh, for heaven's sake," I said, clutching my chest. "Is everyone trying to keep me on edge tonight?"

I placed Van on the floor and checked out the window again. Caleb stood in front of the door, holding Gum Shoe's leash. The German Shepherd danced in anticipation. His thick coat gleamed in the bright sunshine.

I opened the door. "Caleb, what are you doing?"

With a tilt of his head, he gestured toward Gum Shoe. "This guy got away from me and decided to chase a squirrel."

"Uh oh. No squirrel chasing for you, Gum Shoe," I said.

"Who is this?" Mr. Vanderbilt asked as he peered over my shoulder.

Van barked, wanting to get to Gum Shoe. Caleb had no idea that a ghost was staring at him.

"Would you like to come in?" I gestured.

The tiny trailer couldn't hold much more than three people and two dogs. Maybe since Mr. Vanderbilt was a ghost, it wouldn't have such a claustrophobic feel. Caleb peered over my shoulder at Mr. Vanderbilt. Did he see him?

"Sure, I'd love to come in," Caleb said.

He mentioned nothing about Mr. Vanderbilt, so it must have been a coincidence that he looked in his direction. Caleb stepped into the trailer.

Mr. Vanderbilt eyed him up and down. "I assume this is a friend of yours and not the killer . . . or is he a murderer?"

CHAPTER 11

Travel Trailer Tip 11:
For times outside your trailer in the summer
months, use a mixture of two ounces of tea
tree oil in a spray bottle full of water to repel
ticks. This probably won't work to repel
murderers.

Van and Gum Shoe sniffed each other. Van picked up his new chipmunk squeaky toy to show Gum Shoe. I pushed my art supplies out of the way so that Caleb would have a spot to sit down.

"Did you knock on my door a couple minutes ago?" I asked.

If he said no, I'd really freak out.

"Yes, I came by, but that was when Gum Shoe took off. Sorry if I scared you," he said.

I scoffed. "Me? Scared? No way."

He studied my face. "Are you okay?"

"Just peachy," I said through a smile.

"I don't think he believes you," Mr. Vanderbilt said.

"Are you ready for tomorrow?" Caleb asked.

"I'm ready, but just hope the customers are ready."

"Well, I think it was a good thing that they postponed the craft fair for a day," Caleb said. "You can't sell crafts when police are searching for forensic evidence."

"I agree," I said.

Caleb stared over my shoulder, and I knew he was studying the portrait of Mr. Vanderbilt. He stepped around me and up to the painting. Mr. Vanderbilt followed Caleb and stood beside him.

"This is an interesting painting," Caleb said.

"What's that supposed to mean?" Mr. Vanderbilt asked. "Interesting because I'm dashingly handsome?"

"Who is this?" Caleb asked.

"I'm not sure," I said quietly.

My lie was probably evident. Why didn't I just tell him the truth? He knew about the other spirits I'd encountered. Would he be so shocked to discover another one was around? It always worried me that he would think I was crazy each time it happened.

"Really?" Caleb lifted an eyebrow. "I thought maybe you knew him."

"I didn't know him," I said with a smile.

That wasn't a lie. I hadn't known him before the painting.

"You didn't know him?" Caleb asked with confusion.

Darn. I'd hoped he wouldn't pick up on my choice of words. I'd painted myself into a corner.

"Why don't you tell him you know me?" Mr. Vanderbilt asked. "Are you ashamed of me?"

Oh no. I'd upset Mr. Vanderbilt. This was getting worse by the minute. Caleb stared at me, waiting for an answer. Mr. Vanderbilt did the same. I had to come up with some kind of answer. I guess the truth was my only option.

"Okay, I suppose I know him."

A veil of confusion passed over Caleb's face, as if the explanation didn't make sense. The fact that Mr. Vanderbilt was a ghost in our presence hadn't hit him. This was when the idea that I was truly bonkers would settle in.

"Who is it? A relative of yours?" Caleb asked.

I laughed. "No."

"Well, tell the young man. Don't keep him in suspense," Mr. Vanderbilt said.

"That is William Vanderbilt, the builder of the Biltmore Mansion." I gestured.

After saying it out loud, it didn't sound so ridiculous. Maybe I was just painting him because I was here at the Biltmore. Yes, that was it. I would let Caleb believe that, though I would feel bad about not being completely honest with him. Ugh. I was confused.

"Yes, of course. I should have recognized him. I guess you saw a portrait of him in the mansion and decided to paint from memory? You have such talent."

"I didn't see the painting when I was inside the mansion," I said.

"Oh, you found his photo online?" Caleb asked.

"Whatever that means," Mr. Vanderbilt said.

"I didn't check online, either." I watched Caleb's face for a reaction.

Understandably, he seemed confused.

"Okay, I'm out of ideas. How did the painting come about?" Caleb asked.

I shrugged. "I guess you could say it just came to me."

It was then, I thought, that it hit Caleb.

He peered around the room. "I thought I sensed some-

thing. There's a ghost here? The ghost of William Vanderbilt?"

I nodded. "Yes. Do you believe me?"

Caleb ran his hand through his hair. "Wow. Yes, of
course I believe you, it's just kind of crazy, right?"

"Kind of, yes," I said.

"It's not that crazy," Mr. Vanderbilt said. "I mean, I
don't know why it happened, exactly, but I think it happened for a reason."

Caleb realized that my attention was turned to someone else in the room he couldn't see.

"He's here? Did he say something?" Caleb whispered.

"He said that he's glad that he's here," I said.

"I heard the Biltmore was haunted by the ghost of Mr.
Vanderbilt," Caleb said. "I guess now we know that's
true."

"Well, it is my home," Mr. Vanderbilt said. "You can't
expect me to leave."

"Is he a friendly ghost or a mean spirit?" Caleb asked.

"Of course, I'm friendly. What do you think I am, some
kind of monster?" Mr. Vanderbilt said with a sweeping
gesture of his arm.

"He's extremely friendly," I said.

"Hmm. But you don't know why he's here?" Caleb
asked.

"Not a clue," Mr. Vanderbilt said.

"Not a clue," I repeated.

"Well, maybe he'll let you know the reason for his
visit soon, or he'll just go back to the spirit world and
leave you alone."

Mr. Vanderbilt scoffed. "You'd like that, wouldn't
you?"

Maybe I needed to shift the conversation.

"There's another reason why you came to see me, isn't there?" I asked.

Caleb shoved his hands into his pockets. "Yes, I suppose there is."

"I hope it's not bad news," I said.

"Based on his facial expressions, I'd say it's not good," Mr. Vanderbilt said.

"We confirmed that it was a homicide," Caleb said with a solemn face.

"I knew it!" I said. "The killer probably walked right by me as I was entering the mansion."

"Such violence," Mr. Vanderbilt said with a shake of his head.

"Did you notice anyone acting suspiciously?" Caleb asked.

I ran through the memories in my mind. "Nothing that stands out to me."

"Think about it. Maybe something will come back to you."

"How was she murdered?" I asked.

"Strangulation. We believe the murder weapon was the velvet rope used to partition off the area," Caleb said.

"So it was a crime of opportunity. The person didn't necessarily come to the mansion to kill her. Perhaps they got into a fight?"

"Good work, detective," Caleb said with a hint of a smile.

"Celeste is as sharp as a tack," Mr. Vanderbilt said.

"Thank you," I said, answering Caleb and Mr. Vanderbilt at the same time.

"One other thing," Caleb said. "Now that we know this is a murder investigation, and I know you're going to start snooping around, I'm asking you not to do that."

I knew my facial expression displayed exactly how I felt. I was incredulous that he would even ask me not to get involved. Did he know me at all? Of course, he knew me, or he wouldn't even bring this up.

"What's the harm in doing a little snooping around?" I asked.

"Considering there was a murder, and you could be killed, I would say that's the harm," Caleb said.

"I agree with Caleb on this," Mr. Vanderbilt said.

"I'm not going to get myself killed," I said.

Caleb turned and walked toward the door. Was he just going to leave and say nothing else? I didn't want to make him mad. Perhaps I should just go along with his request and snoop around behind his back.

"Caleb, are you mad at me?" I asked.

"I don't know why I bothered to even ask you this," he said when he turned to me again.

To be honest, I didn't know why he bothered to ask that, either. But I would keep that comment to myself.

"Okay, if you don't want me to snoop around, I won't snoop around."

"There's a catch, isn't there?" Mr. Vanderbilt said. "Don't believe her, Caleb."

"Are you serious? Or are you just telling me that?" Caleb asked.

I knew my facial expressions would probably give me away again. I really needed to work on that. Fortunately, Caleb couldn't hear Mr. Vanderbilt's comments.

"I'll try my best not to get involved," I said, holding my hand up.

That was the truth. Okay, so it wasn't the truth. It was another lie. I was just full of lies this morning. Tiny mistruths? Stretches of the truth?

"Shame on you, Celeste." Mr. Vanderbilt wiggled his finger.

Caleb ran his hand through his hair once again. "Okay, I suppose that's the best I can ask for. I can't make you not get involved."

"Well, you could help me out a little," I said.

"Help you go into harm's way? I don't think I can do that," Caleb said.

"That's not very positive, Caleb. It's just helping the poor woman who was murdered."

Caleb opened the door. I hated that he was leaving and was possibly upset with me. What could I do to make it better? Other than not investigate this crime? Pierce would undoubtedly feel the same as Caleb. I would just have to be as sneaky about this as possible. Which was a good thing, anyway. The killer wouldn't know I was on their trail, either.

CHAPTER 12

Travel Trailer Tip 12:
Use things that have a double duty. Like
paintings that add beauty to a space and also
provide clues for a murder investigation.

Caleb had gone, and I had to get back to the painting to search for any hidden images. Mr. Vanderbilt was obviously thinking the same thing, because he was already standing beside his portrait.

He pointed at the canvas. "The distraction is over, so you have to check the painting for your secret messages. I'm excited and anxious."

I'd made it halfway to the painting when another knock sounded on the door.

"What is going on around here?" Mr. Vanderbilt tossed up his hands. "What does he want this time?"

Maybe Caleb had returned to tell me not to investigate again. I got the message the first time. But what if he had returned to tell me that we'd investigate together? Wishful thinking? Yeah, probably. After hurrying back to the door, I peeked out the curtain. Pierce stood at the bottom of the steps, waiting for me to open the door. What would Mr. Vanderbilt say about this visit?

I opened the door. "Pierce, I wasn't expecting to see you."

"You certainly have the fellows in love with you," Mr. Vanderbilt said.

I knew he'd have a comment. Just because a man was here didn't mean he was in love with me. Okay, so Pierce and I had a touch of chemistry, too. But nothing had happened between us.

"I just thought I'd stop by to talk. Is it okay if I come inside?" Pierce asked.

Something told me that he was here for the same reason as Caleb.

"Sure, come on inside." I gestured.

"This is going to delay the hunt for the hidden images again," Mr. Vanderbilt said.

Pierce stepped inside my tiny trailer. Van rushed over to his feet, waiting for Pierce to pet him. Pierce reached down and picked him up.

"Another friend?" Mr. Vanderbilt asked as he eyed Pierce up and down. "Van, I thought I was special. I get the impression you love anyone who will rub your belly."

Pierce's attention was focused on me. He had no idea Mr. Vanderbilt was around.

I held my hand up. "Before you say anything, I know why you're here. You don't want me to be involved in the investigation. I understand . . . it's dangerous. The killer could come after me, and I should just let the police do their job. Blah, blah, blah."

"Are you finished?" Pierce asked.

"Yes, I suppose that's all I had to say," I said.

"Good," Pierce said as he rubbed Van's head. "Because that's not what I was going to say at all."

"You weren't?" I asked with a smidgen of confusion.

"No, I wasn't," Pierce said.

"What were you going to say?" I asked.

"I came to tell you the exact opposite, actually." Pierce stared at me.

Was this some kind of trick? Was he playing a prank on me?

"What do you mean?" I asked with a raised eyebrow.

Van peered up at Pierce, as if he were waiting for the answer, too.

"This is interesting," Mr. Vanderbilt said.

"I think we should investigate the murder," Pierce announced.

I chuckled. "You came here just to tease me, huh?"

"I'm completely serious, Celeste. You're a great detective."

"I like this guy." Mr. Vanderbilt pointed. "Though I still think it's questionable if you should search for the killer."

There had to be a catch or a punch line. I refused to believe Pierce was being serious. Caleb had just left and told me the exact opposite. Pierce had always sided with Caleb on this topic. Their strong opinion was that I shouldn't get involved.

"Do you care to explain exactly what you're up to by saying this? You always said you didn't think I should be involved in this kind of stuff," I said.

"I thought about it, and I changed my mind. I realize that you can be an asset to the investigation," Pierce said.

"The detectives here might have something to say about that," I said.

"Since when did you let that stop you?" he asked.

"Well, never, I suppose," I said. "What are you proposing?"

"Proposing?" Mr. Vanderbilt asked in a loud voice. "If there's going to be a wedding, it must be held in the mansion. I insist."

Forgetting to conceal my expressions from Pierce, I scowled at Mr. Vanderbilt. It was hard not to respond to his comment. A wedding? Heavens, no.

"Are you all right?" Pierce asked.

I wasn't ready to explain the ghost situation to him.

"Yes, I'm fine. Like I said, what's your idea?" I raised an eyebrow at Mr. Vanderbilt so he'd notice my use of a different word this time.

The tiny scar above Pierce's eyebrow appeared more noticeable as he squinted in bewilderment, probably wondering why my behavior seemed odd. "I think we should brainstorm over any clues we have. Perhaps over dinner?"

"Very clever, this one," Mr. Vanderbilt said, pointing to Pierce. "He just successfully asked you for a date. Definitely a risky move, though. He must really like you."

Was that Pierce's plan all along? Just so I would go to dinner with him? Maybe he felt if he'd just asked, I would have said no because of Caleb.

"I guess we could do that," I said. "When did you have in mind?"

"How about now?" Pierce flashed his dazzling smile.

It had been a busy day, and I still hadn't gotten the chance to search for hidden images in the painting. I really wanted to take a peek before I went anywhere.

"Could you give me a few minutes?" I asked.

"Sure, absolutely," Pierce said. "I'll just wait around outside for you."

I smiled. "Thank you."

When Pierce stepped out of the trailer, Mr. Vanderbilt said, "Nice man. I think you two will be very happy together. Your children will be lovely."

"What? Mr. Vanderbilt, we're not getting married."

"You're not?" He massaged his temples, apparently feeling a ghostly headache. "Well, we'll see about that."

I shook my head and stood in front of his portrait. Now maybe I'd find the hidden images.

I picked up the glass and scanned the portrait. Sometimes the images were hard to find. It was as if they really wanted me to work at finding them.

"What do you see?" Mr. Vanderbilt asked as he leaned closer and peered over my shoulder.

After a few seconds, I said, "Aha."

"What did you find?" Mr. Vanderbilt asked excitedly.

"There are two skeletons. One is taking something from the other."

"What is the one taking?" he asked.

"It's not clear. It's just a red blob," I said.

"Why are they skeletons, and why isn't the message clearer?"

"I don't have answers to any of that. I wish I knew. I have to assume it's a message about the murder. Maybe someone was taking something from her. I'll have to ask Pierce if the police think it was a robbery."

"So you're going to work with him after all?" Mr. Vanderbilt asked.

"I can hardly refuse, right? I'd better take advantage before he changes his mind."

Mr. Vanderbilt motioned toward the door. "You'd better get ready. He'll be outside waiting for you."

"Right. I'd almost forgotten." I picked up my purse.

"How could you forget something as important as that?" Mr. Vanderbilt shook his head.

"Be a good boy while I'm gone, Van," I said, kissing him on the forehead. "You be good, too, Mr. Vanderbilt. Goodbye."

"Goodbye? This isn't goodbye. I'm coming with you." Mr. Vanderbilt followed me to the door.

I groaned as I started down the stairs of my trailer. I was afraid he'd say that. Having him talking was distracting, and I'd have a hard time hiding that from Pierce. Speaking of Pierce, he was standing at the side of the trailer. He peered out over the open space toward the mansion. He had no idea that I was walking up behind him. Should I say something? I didn't want to startle him. He still had no idea I'd approached, and I currently stood directly behind him.

"Are you going to stand behind me and not speak?" Pierce asked as he turned around.

"Oh, I didn't know you knew I was here," I said in shock.

"He must have eyes in the back of his head," Mr. Vanderbilt said. "Another sign of a good detective."

We headed across the way toward Pierce's new black Mustang. My dad would love this car. Pierce looked like a Mustang guy, while Caleb seemed like the boy next door in his pickup truck. I still couldn't believe that Pierce and I would be working together. What would Caleb say when he found out? I knew he wouldn't like the idea, considering he'd just told me I shouldn't be involved in the investigation. I needed to ask Pierce more about why he had such a change of heart on that. Pierce and I got into his car and buckled our seat belts. Mr. Vanderbilt sat in the back seat.

"I saw a great place around the corner," Pierce said, starting the car.

"I'm sure I'll love it," I said.

What would we talk about on our drive and while we were eating? Would it be a conversation only about the investigation? Or would we discuss other things? I suppose I would just see where it went. Would Pierce want to talk about anything else? Would that make this a date?

"Are you excited for the craft fair?" he asked. "Even though it definitely got off to a terrible start."

"Obviously, the murder was tragic, but to cancel would've been terrible for so many people who came from so far away to enjoy it," I said.

"Well, I'm excited to see your work," he said.

"And I can't wait to see yours. You've been so secretive about it."

This conversation was easier than I thought. So maybe we wouldn't only discuss the murder investigation. Oh no. What if this really was a date? Mr. Vanderbilt was being suspiciously quiet as he stared out the window. I got the impression he was pretending not to listen to us.

"I'm just a little nervous about my work, and I don't know the right time to show anyone," he said.

"I'm sure it's great," I said with a smile.

Up ahead, I recognized a building. It was the one I had seen Deidre visit. The one where I had the confrontation with the stocky man. As we grew closer, I realized there was a sign out front. I couldn't wait to see what it said.

BLUE RIDGE MOUNTAINS ART GALLERY.

Interesting. I knew for sure the sign hadn't been there before.

CHAPTER 13

Travel Trailer Tip 13:
Look for hidden nooks and crannies for extra
storage space.

"Can you stop the car?" I asked.

Pierce eased off the gas pedal. "Sure. Is something wrong?"

"Can you pull over right here?" I pointed toward the curb. "I need to check out this place."

"Oh no. Not this place again," Mr. Vanderbilt said, finally speaking up. "I don't like it here."

Pierce pulled over to the side of the road.

"The art gallery here? If they're open, we can go in," Pierce said.

"I'd like that," I said. "I don't think they're open yet."

On the bottom of the large sign was a smaller, temporary one that read COMING SOON.

"Well, hopefully they'll be open before we leave town, and we can come back if you'd like," he said.

"Sure . . . I guess," I said.

"Is something bothering you? Are you sure everything's all right?" Pierce asked.

"Aren't you going to tell him what happened here?" Mr. Vanderbilt asked. "That's awfully deceptive of you."

"Well, it isn't the art that makes me want to come back here," I said.

Mr. Vanderbilt tossed his hands up. "It's about time you told him. Thank you!"

He was being dramatic.

"Really?" Pierce asked with a raised eyebrow. "Why do you say that?"

"I suppose since we're doing this investigation together, I can tell you this."

"Go on," Pierce said.

"I followed a woman to this building. That sign wasn't out here. She went inside with a man. And I just happened to sneak around the side of the building and listen in on their conversation."

"That's not all," Mr. Vanderbilt said. "Don't leave out any of the facts."

"Just happened to listen to their conversation, huh?" Pierce asked.

"The man wasn't happy with her. Actually, he even grabbed her, and she took off. He wanted something from her. He told her that she'd better have it soon. The worst part, though, was that the man caught me snooping."

"What happened after that?"

"I ran around the side of the building. I was hoping to get back to my truck."

"And did you?" Pierce asked with anticipation.

"Well, obviously," I said with a chuckle.

Pierce laughed. "Right, I see that, but what I meant is did you get back safely? Did he hurt you at all? I need to have a talk with him. Where can I find him? Do you know his name? What does he look like?"

Pierce was full of questions.

After describing the man, I said, "I wish I knew where to find him, other than here at this building. That's why I want to come back when they're open."

"Tell me exactly what the man said," Pierce said.

"I didn't make it back to the truck without a confrontation with him, that's for sure."

"What did he do?" Pierce asked.

"He wanted to know what I was doing there, of course. I told him that I was searching for my dog. That Van had run off. Luckily, I had Van with me to back up that story."

"That's a relief," Pierce said. "But extremely dangerous."

Oh no. Was he changing his mind about working together on this?

"He's certainly right about it being dangerous," Mr. Vanderbilt said.

"Yes, it is dangerous, but I handled it just fine. The man was highly suspicious, to say the least. If he sees me back here again, he'll know I was up to something."

"Well, I'll be with you next time. I want to ask him some questions. Who's the woman that was here talking to him, and why were you following her?"

"Deidre Ashley. She's a friend of the murdered woman. I got that information from someone who works at the mansion."

Pierce smiled. "Of course you did. The police probably haven't even talked to her."

"Well, that's what I'm here for," I said with a wink.

"I think this is a bad idea," Mr. Vanderbilt said as he popped up from the back seat.

He startled me with the sudden movement, and I jumped.

"Is everything all right?" Pierce asked.

I couldn't explain that there was a ghost in the back seat who had just scared me. I had to come up with a logical explanation as to why I had that crazy reaction.

I pointed straight ahead. "Oh, I thought I saw the man and that startled me, but it was just a shadow."

Pierce followed my pointing finger. "I guess you're just antsy about talking about him again after what happened."

"Yes, that's it exactly," I said.

"You should just tell him that I'm here," Mr. Vanderbilt said.

No way was I doing that. I had enough problems.

Pierce moved the car's gearshift into drive and said, "We should go ahead to the restaurant."

"Absolutely," I said, giving the building one last glance before we pulled away.

Since I had the name of the new art gallery, I could research online and find out who was responsible for it and if that was the same man who I had encountered here.

We'd barely gotten away from the building when a red Corvette zipped out from a side entrance ahead of us. I caught a glimpse of the driver as he turned out onto the main road.

"I'm pretty sure that was the man I encountered here," I said, pointing at the car.

"What?" Mr. Vanderbilt popped up from the back again.

"Are you serious?" Pierce asked.

"I'm almost positive," I said.

He pushed on the gas just to catch up with the car. We were right behind him.

"Well, we're going to follow him and see if we can get to the bottom of this," Pierce said.

"What should we do?" I asked as we rolled up to a stoplight.

Pierce picked up his phone. "I know one thing I'm going to do."

Pierce touched the screen to place a call. He put the phone up to his ear.

"I'm curious," Mr. Vanderbilt said.

He wasn't the only one who wondered what Pierce was up to. I was still shocked that I'd spotted the man in his car.

"I need some information on a license plate," Pierce said to the person on the other end of the line.

Wow, that was convenient. All he had to do was place a call.

"I hope he finds information on this person," Mr. Vanderbilt said.

I would love to have a name. That would help us a lot. Maybe Pierce and I made a great team. However, I thought Caleb and I made a great team, too. I was so torn. I didn't know what to think. I waited anxiously for Pierce to fill me in on the details of the call. In the meantime, I focused on the car ahead of us. I wondered if the man would recognize me if he saw me in his rearview mirror. We had been close to each other when he grabbed me. The light turned green, and we took off behind the Corvette.

Pierce ended the call. "I got what I needed."

"What did you find out?" I asked with wide eyes in anticipation.

"His name is Stan Knowles. I have the address, so if we happen to lose him, we can go to his house."

"Can you do that?" I asked. "You know, since this isn't your investigation."

"Would you let that stop you?" he asked.

"No, I suppose I wouldn't," I said with a sly smile.

"Well, you have your answer."

"That is a nifty trick he has," Mr. Vanderbilt said. "All he has to do is talk into that contraption and get information he needs on the car in front of him. My, how times have changed."

Yes, they had changed, but some things never changed . . . like murder. And I was determined to figure out who had committed this horrific crime.

"I suppose it'll be kind of awkward just to go up to this man and ask why he was talking to Deidre Ashley. Especially considering we don't know her," I said.

Pierce tapped his fingers against the steering wheel as we trailed the man's car. "I have to think of something. You're right, though. We can't come right out and ask him questions about the woman, because he'll freak out and not answer."

Mirroring Pierce's movements, I drummed my fingers against the leather seat.

"How about you ask him about the art gallery?" Mr. Vanderbilt asked as he leaned forward from the back seat again.

"That's a good idea," I said, forgetting not to answer him in front of Pierce.

Pierce raised an eyebrow. "What's a good idea?"

I chuckled. "I was thinking of a good idea in my head and forgot to say it out loud."

He laughed. "Well, all right, let's hear it."

I would have to be more careful about what I said in front of Pierce if Mr. Vanderbilt was talking in my ear.

"We can pretend to be interested in the art gallery. We can ask him some questions about the art. However . . ." I said. "The only problem is Stan Knowles already saw me, so I can't exactly question him. He'll be too suspicious if he sees me again."

"That's true," Mr. Vanderbilt said. "I thought of that. I just forgot to say it."

"Therefore, you have to do this on your own," I said.

Jealousy set in. I wanted to question Stan and not let Pierce do it on his own. I wanted to be involved, though I had to realize that I couldn't do everything. Unless I came up with a different plan, it would have to be this way. At this time, I had nothing else.

"I suppose I could do that," Pierce said. "But I'm not sure what I would ask about the art gallery. I'm not exactly an art expert. I've only just started working with my medium."

I sensed Pierce's uneasiness at the thought of talking to Stan, but Pierce was a detective, and I assumed he would be just fine.

Stan made a right turn. Pierce stayed back just a hair before making the turn, as well.

"I hope he doesn't realize we're following him. But when we show up at his place, he might figure it out," I said.

"You guys are two of the greatest people I've ever known. You're really going for this murder investigation," Mr. Vanderbilt said.

Stan made another left turn onto the street that was listed as his address.

"This is the street you said, right?" I asked.

"Yes, this is it," Pierce said.

Stan slowed down. I wasn't sure if that was because he

was nearing his house or whether he realized we were following him. Soon, he turned into a driveway for a large brick ranch.

"I'm glad we had his address. Otherwise, there's no telling whose house we would've arrived at," Mr. Vanderbilt said.

"He must live here," I said.

Pierce pulled the car up to the curb and shoved it into park. We watched as Stan got out of his car and headed toward the front door.

"Do you have a plan?" I asked. We watched the man as he got out his keys and unlocked the front door.

The shiny gold keychain caught the sunlight and glinted against the pavement.

"Not really," Pierce said. "I guess I'll just wing it."

"That seems to be the best thing to me."

Pierce and I had another thing in common. That was the way I did things, too.

"Winging it makes me nervous," Mr. Vanderbilt said.

Pierce shut off the car. "Okay, I'm going in. If I'm not out in a while, come for me."

"Are you serious?"

He chuckled. "No, of course I'll come out. Actually, I am serious, if I don't come out after a while, come for me or call the police for backup."

"I don't like you joking like that," I said.

He handed me the keys.

"What's this for?" I asked.

"In case we need a quick getaway. Perhaps you should get behind the wheel," Pierce said.

"What do you plan on doing in there?" Mr. Vanderbilt asked.

I took the keys reluctantly and watched as Pierce got

out of the car and headed up the path toward the front door. I got out of the car, too, and then scrambled behind the steering wheel. Maybe this was more dangerous than I thought. It wasn't as if we were robbing the house, so why did I have to be the getaway driver?

Pierce reached the front door and rang the doorbell. It was a matter of seconds before the door opened and Stan Knowles was standing in front of Pierce. They talked, and Stan motioned for Pierce to step inside. This made me even more anxious.

Pierce checked over his shoulder, and I wondered if that was some kind of signal. Did he want me to save him? No, probably not. He walked inside, and Stan closed the door. That set off even more of a panic, because I couldn't see what was going on in the house.

"What do we do while we wait?" Mr. Vanderbilt asked.

"We wait," I said, fidgeting in the seat.

"That seems kind of boring."

"Yes, it is boring, but it's not as if we can leave," I said.

"Of course not, but maybe we can chitchat. You know, to take our minds off the anxiety."

"You can chitchat all you want, Mr. Vanderbilt, but I'm not sure how chatty I will be. When I get nervous, I tend to be quiet." I tapped my fingers against the steering wheel.

"Turn on the radio. Music would be good to lighten the mood," he said.

I flipped on the radio to the oldies station. We sat in silence as we watched the house. Ten minutes had gone by, and I wasn't sure how long was too long to wait. Pierce hadn't said an exact time to come for him. Was it ten minutes? Fifteen? Thirty, or an hour?

Twenty minutes slipped by. And another ten. Thirty minutes was way too long with no sign of him. Maybe if I could just peek in a window, I wouldn't have to knock on the door.

I unbuckled my seat belt. "Okay, I'm going out there."

"Are you sure this is a good idea?" Mr. Vanderbilt asked.

"No, I'm not sure, but nevertheless, I have to do it."

I opened the car door and walked around to the front of the car. Mr. Vanderbilt joined me. Staring at the house, I wondered if I should go to the front door or maybe just check in one of the side windows. I assumed they probably had moved into the living room or the kitchen. Not knowing the layout of the house, I didn't know where those rooms would be, but based on the window placement, I assumed the living room was to the left of the front door, and the kitchen would probably be in the back. I would take a peek in the front windows first. The blinds were open, but since it was light out, I wasn't sure how much I would be able to see into the house from the outside.

Like a cat burglar, I inched across the front lawn. Mr. Vanderbilt was behind me. When I reached the windows, I pressed my back against the brick wall of the house.

"What are you waiting on?" Mr. Vanderbilt asked.

"I have to mentally prepare myself," I said. "On the count of three, I'm going to peek over into the window."

"Should I count to three, or are you counting to three?"

"I'll handle the counting," I said.

In my mind, I counted down. When I reached three, I

eased over and peered into the window. I had to press my face right up against the glass, which made me nervous. What if they were in there, and Pierce saw me? He wouldn't be able to explain that, and Stan would obviously recognize me right away. It took a while for my eyes to adjust. No one was in the room.

I moved away from the window and stood on the porch like the confused amateur sleuth that I was.

"Well, what are you going to do?" Mr. Vanderbilt asked.

"I don't know," I said. "I guess I'll have to knock on the door."

"This probably isn't going to end well," he said.

"Thank you, but I don't need that reminder."

I knew that this wasn't a good thing, but my mind was playing tricks on me. I was thinking of all the worst-case scenarios. This man had been awfully mean to Deidre and me, so I assumed he was probably being that way to Pierce, as well. Of course, I knew that Pierce could take care of himself. Nevertheless, sometimes people got into situations that they just couldn't get out of, no matter how strong, tough, or smart they were. I stood in front of the door, preparing myself to pound on it. I'd just raised my hand to knock when a crash sounded from outside.

CHAPTER 14

Travel Trailer Tip 14:
Use all the space, inside and out.

"What was that?" Mr. Vanderbilt asked.

"I don't know," I said, "but it sounded as if it came from around the side of the house. I suppose I have to check it out."

My anxiety spiked as I moved away from the front door and over to the side of the house. I had no idea what to expect. This was making me even more afraid for Pierce. When Mr. Vanderbilt and I reached the edge of the home, I paused.

"What are you waiting for?" he asked. "Detective Pierce could be in danger."

"What if he is in danger? How will I help him?"

"You'll think of something," Mr. Vanderbilt said. "Go. Do you want me to check it out?"

"What good would that do?" I asked.

I peeked around the side of the house. I saw no one out

there. With adrenaline rushing through me, I eased around the side of the house and headed for the back. If I didn't see anything back there, I would have to return to the front door and knock. I'd break the door down if I had to. How I would achieve that, I had no clue.

Once again, Mr. Vanderbilt and I reached the end of the house. As I paused, I raised my hand, instructing Mr. Vanderbilt to do the same. As if it really mattered if he walked past the edge of the house. No one would see him.

"Oh no. Not this again. You're wasting time," Mr. Vanderbilt said.

"Yes, I know. You told me that repeatedly."

When I peeked around the side of the house into the backyard, I saw a man. It wasn't Pierce, and it wasn't Stan. Who was this, and what was he doing? Should I say something?

"Who is that?" Mr. Vanderbilt whispered in my ear.

"I wish I knew," I said.

"Are you going to ask him?"

"I haven't decided what I'm doing yet. Give me a second to think."

Before I had a chance to contemplate further, the man turned his attention my way. Our eyes locked.

"Is everything okay?" he asked.

At least he didn't come after me. I stared at the man in stunned silence.

"Ask him where's Detective Pierce," Mr. Vanderbilt said.

"Do you live here?" I managed to ask.

"I'm just here to trim the hedges," he said. "Would you like me to get the owner for you?"

"Oh no, that's not necessary," I said.

That was the last thing I wanted. I still had to find Pierce. The man stared for a few more seconds before turning and walking over to his landscaping equipment.

"You should have told him to get the owner," Mr. Vanderbilt said.

"Maybe I should have, but that's neither here nor there," I said.

I stepped back from the edge of the house. I suppose I would have to return to the front door. When someone tapped me on the shoulder, I screamed, which caused Mr. Vanderbilt to scream, too. I spun around to see who was behind me. *Please don't let it be a murderer.*

"What are you doing, Celeste?" Pierce asked.

I relaxed my tense shoulders, glad that I had found him. "I was searching for you."

"In the backyard?" he asked with a raised eyebrow.

"Well, I heard a noise, so I came to check it out. I was really worried about you. What took so long?"

"Oh, I had a long chat with Mr. Knowles."

"What did you find out?" I asked. "Is he the killer?"

"Well, I didn't get a confession out of him, if that's what you want to know. We should get back in the car, and I'll explain." Pierce motioned.

We headed down the side of the house toward the car.

"I thought you were going to wait in the car for me," he said.

"You knew that was never going to happen," I said.

Pierce and I got back into the car, with Mr. Vanderbilt easily slipping right through the car into the back seat.

I buckled my seat belt. "Okay, tell me what happened. I have to know."

"I had a conversation with Mr. Knowles and asked him about the art gallery. I told him that I was an investor and wanted to donate."

"Oh, that is so deceitful," I said. "But I like it."

He laughed. "I couldn't tell him I wanted to display my artwork in there. He would tell me to get lost. So I had to come up with another reason."

"Did you ask him if he murdered the woman?" Mr. Vanderbilt asked from the back seat.

"Did you ask about the murder?" I asked.

I knew I should have gone inside with him. I would have all the details. I hated getting them after the fact.

"Well, I casually mentioned the Biltmore," he said. "That gave me a reason to discuss the murder."

"Good thinking," Mr. Vanderbilt said.

"He denied knowing Deidre or the murder victim. Obviously, he has something to hide," Pierce said as he made a left turn.

"You need to get to the bottom of this," Mr. Vanderbilt said. "Of course, don't get yourself killed in the process."

"How will we find out what he's keeping from us? I think we should speak with Deidre," I said.

"I'll do that as soon as possible," Pierce said.

I held up my hand. "What do you mean, you'll speak with her? I thought we were doing this together?"

"We are doing this together. It's just that if things get dangerous . . ."

"I see how this is going. You say we're in this together, but we're really not," I said.

"Oh, boy." Mr. Vanderbilt leaned back in the seat, trying to distance himself from the conversation.

"That's not it," Pierce said.

"Suddenly I'm not that hungry," I said.

"I'm sorry, Celeste, you're right. We are investigating together," Pierce said.

Mr. Vanderbilt and I remained silent. I sensed he felt the same as me. I'd give Pierce another chance, but I wasn't sure I believed him.

CHAPTER 15

Travel Trailer Tip 15:
Bring only the necessities for the trip. If
you have to leave in a hurry, you'll want
to travel light.

After we ate, Pierce dropped me off at the estate. We hadn't discussed the investigation further over our meal. I'd shifted the conversation, because I was still upset with him. I just needed some time to get over it. Arriving back at my trailer, I spotted a police presence. Had there been another murder? If so, I would have to reconsider staying for the craft fair. That would be entirely too dangerous.

Around the corner from my trailer, I noticed the manager, Daisy Harmon, who had coordinated the craft fair. Daisy tucked strands of her almond-brown hair behind her ear. She must have done that ten times on the day I'd spoken with her about a booth at the fair. Perhaps it was a nervous tic. She was speaking with the employee I had met earlier. I recognized Cheryl, because she wore the same navy-blue uniform and thick eyeglasses. I'd love to talk with Cheryl again. Maybe she could tell me what was going on with the police being here.

I busied myself with organizing some of my display items while I waited for Daisy and Cheryl to finish talking. An overwhelming urge to paint overcame me. I hoped that meant I would paint another hidden image that would provide a clue to finding the murderer. However, I had to catch Cheryl before she got away, so the painting would have to wait just a little longer.

After a few more minutes, the women ended their conversation and headed in opposite directions, so I hurried for the employee, hoping to catch her before she got away.

Once I was close enough, I called out to her, "Excuse me."

Cheryl turned around right away and focused her dark-eyed gaze on me.

I think it took her a second to realize who I was, but she said, "Oh, hello. How are you?"

"I'm all right," I said. "I was just wondering why there's such a police presence. Did something else happen? Please tell me it wasn't a murder."

She shook her head. "No, but a priceless painting was stolen from the mansion."

"Are you serious? Which painting? A Renoir? A Monet?"

"A Sargent painting that George Vanderbilt commissioned of Frederick Law Olmsted."

"How did that happen?"

Artwork played a role in Biltmore history. I'd learned about the top-secret Biltmore Estate room that had been used to store valuable art during World War II. George and Edith Vanderbilt had always held an appreciation for the arts.

"They're not sure, exactly. The burglar was very stealthy and managed to escape being captured on video, which is very difficult."

"I imagine it is. However, someone also managed to murder Ellen McDonald off camera, as well. And get away with it. It's almost as if the person has intimate knowledge of where the cameras are and the angles."

"I don't know about that," she said. "They could just be lucky."

It didn't seem like luck to me, but I wouldn't debate the fact with her.

"I wonder if the person who took the painting is the same person who murdered Ellen. Why wouldn't they have taken the painting when they murdered her?" I asked.

"That doesn't seem likely." She scowled. "It's probably a coincidence."

"Perhaps they didn't have time, and they had to get out of there. It could've been a heated argument between them, and the person murdered Ellen without intending. It wasn't premeditated, in other words. They came back for the painting."

She crossed her arms in front of her. I took it that she was skeptical of my theory. But it was just that—a theory—and I had absolutely no clues to lead me in that direction. I could be completely off base. I'd been known to get things wrong a time or two. Okay, I'd been wrong a bunch of times. She seemed more reluctant to talk to me now. I wasn't sure what had changed. But something had happened.

She gestured over her shoulder. "Well, I should get back to work now."

"Right. Sorry for holding you up," I said.

"Oh, it's all right," she said with a forced smile. "I'll see you later."

She turned around and headed across the way. I stood there, thinking about what she had said. I just felt confident that the murder and the robbery were connected.

"That seems suspicious," Mr. Vanderbilt said from over my shoulder.

I clutched my chest. "Oh, I forgot you were there."

"How could you forget about me?" he asked.

"What do you mean, 'that seems suspicious'?"

"She acted as if what you said wasn't valid. I think you may be on to something."

"Well, maybe she's just not that suspicious like I am, but I think the missing portrait and the murder are connected."

"I don't see how you couldn't come to that conclusion," Mr. Vanderbilt said.

"I wonder what the others will think of this," I said.

"You have to let them know right away and find out."

"I think someone with inside knowledge of the mansion took the painting."

"What if it was that employee you were just talking to?" Mr. Vanderbilt asked.

"Cheryl? The thought had crossed my mind," I said.

"What thought crossed your mind? I heard that you are investigating with a partner," a different voice said.

I whipped around to find Caleb standing behind me. I knew this time would come eventually.

"I wouldn't say that we're partners, per se," I said.

"What do you mean?" Caleb asked.

"It's just that Pierce said we would investigate this together. But now he wants to keep me from being a part of it, because he thinks it's dangerous."

"I told you I thought it was dangerous from the beginning, but you didn't listen to me," Caleb said.

I raised an eyebrow. "I think I won't listen to you or Pierce."

"You tell him, Celeste," Mr. Vanderbilt said with a bump of his fist.

I turned and headed back toward my trailer, leaving Caleb standing in the same spot. Mr. Vanderbilt walked beside me. He mumbled something about Caleb, but I was too frustrated with Caleb to pay attention.

"Celeste," Caleb called out.

I ignored him and continued toward the trailer. Pierce and Caleb both needed to take some time and reflect on their actions. When they came to their senses, I would speak with them. I would investigate this crime if I wanted . . . and right now, I very much wanted to investigate. Not only did I have to figure out the murder, but also who took the painting. That would be no easy task.

I stepped into my trailer and peeked out the window to see if Caleb was still standing back there. He watched the trailer for a few seconds before heading in the opposite direction. I hated having tension between us, but it was unavoidable, as long as Pierce and Caleb continued to act this way.

Van raced over to me.

I picked him up and hugged him. "I missed you, too."

"So nice to have the unconditional love of a dog," Mr. Vanderbilt said.

After several licks, Van squirmed in my arms.

"I know what you want. It's time for your treat," I said, placing Van back onto the floor.

My interest was still on Stan Knowles and Deidre Ashley. What were they up to, and how did they know each other? He was an art dealer and knew Ellen's best friend. Coincidentally, a painting was stolen from the mansion.

I handed Van a bacon-flavored doggie treat. He finished it in under three seconds and stared at me to see if I wanted to give him more.

"That's all for right now, Van," I said. "We have crimes to investigate. I smell a rat, and his name is likely Stan. Do you want to help me catch a rat, Van?"

He barked and wagged his tail. Mr. Vanderbilt laughed.

Stan likely knew of someone who would pay him a lot of money for that painting. If Ellen tried to stop him from taking the painting, that would certainly be a motive for Stan to murder her. I needed to get Stan to confess or find solid evidence that he was the murderer. How I would do this was still a big unknown.

While I needed to find out who had perpetrated this horrendous crime, I also had to get to work with the craft fair. I had a short time to set up my art and get ready for the customers. Plus, I wanted to paint. I'd try to squeeze that in during the downtime between customers. Well, I hoped to have so many customers that I was searching for downtime. What if I had not a single customer at all? I would have plenty of time for my painting.

Painting was at the top of my to-do list, because I wanted to see if another hidden image came through. I needed any help I could get with finding clues. As far as I was concerned, I was on my own with this investigation. I set out my paintings neatly around the outside of the trailer. Even though it was daylight, the string of twinkling lights on my trailer cast a lovely glow across the art.

As I was moving Mr. Vanderbilt's picture, he said, "Wait a minute. What are you doing with that? You're not selling me, are you? I thought you would want to keep my picture around for always."

"Of course, I'm not selling your portrait, Mr. Vanderbilt. I'm just setting it aside so that no one buys it."

"Well, all right," he said. "But you might want to hide it, because somebody will come along and want to buy it. They may offer you such a great price that you won't be able to refuse."

I chuckled. "You're right. Maybe I should put it inside so no one will see it."

I hated to break it to him, but I wasn't sure that my art was at that level quite yet. People wouldn't pay huge prices for my work, even a portrait of him. I placed a new canvas on the easel with my paints all set out and ready. People were starting to trickle into the fairgrounds, and I hoped that I would sell some of my art early. Painting while they walked by would, with any luck, attract attention. However, when a ruckus came from nearby, I knew they wouldn't pay attention to me. I saw a security guard wrestling with a petite, dark-haired woman. She pushed the muscular man and darted to her right, but he quickly grabbed her before she got away. Shockingly, the sleeve of her Biltmore Estate uniform had ripped from the shoulder's seams.

"Wow, what's going on there?" Mr. Vanderbilt asked.

"I don't know what happened," I said.

"Oh, that woman was fired."

I didn't know that someone was standing close enough

to hear me talking. Once again, I needed to watch my talking to Mr. Vanderbilt. People would think I was crazy.

"She worked here at the estate?" I asked.

The slightly built woman with caramel-colored hair hadn't noticed that I hadn't been talking to her. I recognized her as another vendor. She sold bracelets with tiger-eye and obsidian beads.

"Yes, she did," the woman said.

"There's quite a bit of action happening today, not to mention the horrible event from the other day," I said.

This woman probably had no idea that I was the one who discovered the murder victim.

The woman gestured, showcasing her arm full of earthy-colored bracelets. "Yes, I don't know what's going on, but there's been a lot of turmoil around here. It's scary. I heard that this woman was stealing things."

"What type of things? Was she the one who took the painting?"

"I hope they recover the painting," Mr. Vanderbilt said.

I would be shocked if it turned out that she took the painting and not Stan Knowles.

"I don't think she took the painting. Well, not that I know of, at least, but I suppose if she took something else, she may have taken the painting, as well. She's probably a suspect, and that's why they're taking her away from the premises."

"What did she take?" I asked.

"I heard it was money."

"So not actual items, but cash?"

"I think she was stealing from other employees," the woman said.

"Wow, this is an interesting turn of events. Thank you for the information," I said.

She raised an eyebrow. "You're welcome."

She seemed confused by my comment. I suppose it appeared as if I were investigating a crime. That was because I *was* investigating a crime. I turned my attention back to my art. There were no customers right now. Everyone was preoccupied with watching the commotion. This certainly wouldn't help the craft fair if everyone thought it was full of chaos and crime.

Deciding to use this opportunity to focus on my painting, I sat down in front of the canvas and picked up my brush. As I dabbed the tip of the brush into the blue-sky color, I let my imagination go. The next thing I knew, without even realizing, I was brushing strokes across the blank canvas.

"I can't wait to see what it is," Mr. Vanderbilt said from over my shoulder.

I wasn't used to working with an audience standing so close.

"Do you already have the image in your mind? Can you tell me what it is?" he pressed.

"I don't have the image at all. It just comes to me as I'm painting," I said.

"That's fascinating."

The painting was taking shape surprisingly fast. Within a short time, the scene was basically the same as how I imagined it was right before the murder occurred. When Ellen was still working, and everything was fine with her life. But was there a hidden image? I certainly hoped so, because without that, this painting was just nothing more than an innocent painting.

"That's inside the mansion," Mr. Vanderbilt said.

"Yes, the room where I found Ellen. I assume this is a short time before she was murdered."

"Is there one of the hidden images that you described?" Mr. Vanderbilt asked.

"Well, there's only one way to find out," I said.

An empty glass jar sat nearby just for this purpose. I knew if anyone saw me holding the jar to my eye and studying the painting, they would think I was bonkers. Nevertheless, I held the jar up to my eye and stared at the painting. It took a bit of scanning to find the hidden image, but it was there. Just as I had hoped.

My adrenaline was pumping as I stared at a pair of skeletons. I had to make out what this image meant. Were the two skeletons arguing? It was hard to understand what this meant. One skeleton was considerably taller than the other. I suppose that was a clue, but what?

"What do you see?" Mr. Vanderbilt asked excitedly.

"There are two skeletons. One is much taller than the other. And they seem to be arguing," I said.

"How can you tell?" he asked.

"Well, one is pointing at the other one, who is holding its hands up. I think that stance is like they are angry with each other. One is more fearful than the other."

"Do you think that's an image of the killer arguing with Ellen?" Mr. Vanderbilt asked.

"It seems that way," I said.

"Psst," a voice said.

Caleb was peeking around the side of my trailer.

"Do I need a white flag of surrender?" he asked.

That made me grin.

"No, you don't," I said, placing the jar down.

He stepped out from behind the trailer and over to me. Right away, he noticed the painting.

"Painting the crime scene now, are you?"

"Well, it's not exactly the crime scene, since there's been no crime yet in the painting." I pointed.

"Is this another one of the paintings with the hidden images?" he asked.

I handed him the glass jar. "Would you like to take a gander for yourself?"

He studied my face. "I suppose I would, yes."

I moved out of the way so that Caleb could get a clear view of the painting as he peered through the glass.

Caleb scanned the painting before moving the glass away from his eye. "I see it. That's very odd. What do you think it means?"

"My guess is it's showing the argument between Ellen and her murderer. The only thing that gives me a clue to the identity of the killer is that the person is much taller than her. Stan Knowles would be much taller than her," I said.

"Well, it's certainly a clue, but nothing that would lead to an arrest."

"No, but it means that I can pursue Stan even harder, I suppose."

He handed me the glass back. "Just because I was ready to wave the white flag doesn't mean that I don't think this is still dangerous. But if you are determined to go on with investigating, at least I can be with you to help."

"Are you going to be like Pierce and say that you want to help but don't want me to be involved because it's dangerous?" I placed a hand on my right hip.

"No, absolutely not," he said, holding up his hands.

I wasn't sure if I believed him.

"Surely with two detectives helping, you can track down the murderer," Mr. Vanderbilt said.

I'd like to think that was the case, but Pierce and Caleb might be more of a hindrance than a help.

Caleb shoved his hands into his pants pockets. "When do we start? Where is Stan Knowles? And who is he?"

"I have his address, and he's an art dealer. He's opening a gallery. That's why I think he took the painting from the mansion."

"Well, I would think the police will find evidence of that, with all the cameras they have around here."

"Unless he had some inside help," I said.

"That's true," Caleb said.

Any investigating would have to be put on hold, because right now I had customers walking up to my booth. I needed to sell artwork first and investigate crime later. Making a mental note, I reminded myself to check out the disorderly employee who had just been fired. Perhaps she could give me more information or provide some clues. Or maybe she stole the painting. After all, she had been stealing money from the other employees. Or at least she had been accused.

Was she responsible for the murder, as well?

CHAPTER 16

Travel Trailer Tip 16:
Make a list and check it twice. You might for-
get something. Traveling can be stressful . . .
especially if you cross paths with a murderer.

As I packed up my paintings for the day, I sensed some-one watching me. When Van growled, I knew something was amiss. Chills ran up my spine when I thought of the murderer being somewhere hidden and watching me. I picked Van up and tried to soothe him so that he wouldn't be upset. He was out to catch the murderer just as much as I was, apparently.

"You sense that too, huh, Van?" I whispered.

He growled again. I only wished I knew where this person was hiding. I finished putting the paintings away and decided to check the back of the trailer.

With Van still in my arms, I eased around the side of the trailer. No one was watching me or seemed interested in what I was doing, at least not that I saw. Standing at the corner of the trailer, I checked to the left and to the right. Maybe my mind was playing tricks on me.

"I guess there's nothing out of the ordinary, Van. We should get some dinner. What do you say?"

He barked, letting me know that was a great idea. I turned and headed back around the trailer. No one was waiting there for me. That allowed me to calm down.

While Van and I had dinner, I would figure out a way to get the name of the fired employee. Without a name, I couldn't find out more information about her, which I felt was critical in solving the case. As Van and I stepped back into the trailer, I bumped into Mr. Vanderbilt. No matter how much I talked to him or saw him around, when he popped up in front of me like that, it always startled me.

"Oh, I'm sorry," he said, taking a bit of a bow.

"You need to stop doing that." I clutched my chest, trying to get my heart rate to settle down.

"Right. I need to remember not to scare you." Mr. Vanderbilt punctuated the sentence with a point of his finger.

The sun would set soon. I needed to get my sleuthing done before that happened. I wanted to find Cheryl before she left for the day, if possible. Of course, there was no guarantee she would talk to me again, since our last conversation was awkward. I would give it a shot, though.

After we ate, Van wanted a nap. I left him at the trailer. Mr. Vanderbilt was with me as I set off toward the small building that was the employees' office.

"I sure hope you find Cheryl," Mr. Vanderbilt said as he walked beside me.

"Me too," I said. "More importantly, I hope I find out the fired employee's name."

"Well, if she doesn't speak with you, maybe you can find someone else who will."

"Fingers crossed," I said.

The sound of footsteps came from behind me. Checking over my shoulder, I saw no one back there.

"Did you hear that?" I whispered.

"I didn't notice anything," Mr. Vanderbilt said.

"I suppose it was nothing."

I continued toward the office. But the sound came again, and this time when I peeked over my shoulder, I thought I saw someone dart behind a nearby tree. My heart sped up.

"I think someone may be following me," I said.

"Just keep walking," he said.

Was I just imagining this? I hurried my steps and continued toward the office. But panic was starting to set in. What if someone was really following me? What if it was the killer? Pierce and Caleb's voices echoed through my mind—their words of telling me this was too dangerous. Nevertheless, I continued on my way, determined not to give up on my investigation.

I made it to the office area without being attacked. I still saw no signs of anyone following me now. I wasn't sure which door I should go into. The one on the side, or the one in the front? Both appeared the same, and neither was marked. I supposed the one in the front was the main door, so I would pick that one.

Luckily, no one was behind me. Just as I reached the door, though, a noise caught my attention again. When I glanced over my shoulder this time, Cheryl was there.

She was just the person I was searching for. Was she the one who had been following me?

"Hello," I said with a smile. "We meet again."

She grinned. "Yes, we do."

At least she was being pleasant this time. That was a good sign. A few strands of her espresso-colored locks had slipped from her ponytail. A smidge of something yellow stained the front of her uniform's jacket. Was that mustard?

"Did you need something?" she asked.

I hated to tell her that I wanted to find her. That sounded kind of creepy. I wasn't sure why I felt so nervous about asking this, but this woman was a bit intimidating. Not that she would body slam me or anything, but her icy stare sent a chill through my body like a blast from a blizzard. She had been nice at first, but her behavior had switched back and forth between nice and cold.

"I'm looking for the employee who was fired. I mean, I know she's not working here, but I wonder if you know her name."

She stared at me with her icy blue eyes and crossed her arms in front of her. "Are you an undercover detective or something?"

Mr. Vanderbilt chuckled.

"I'm not a detective. I'm just helping my friends who are detectives."

This sounded better than admitting that I was obsessed with finding the killer for the sake of the murder victim. Finding her body had given me a stake in the game. Plus, if the police didn't find the killer at some point, they would turn their attention back to me again as the prime suspect.

"Her name is Tasha Kenmore. That's all I know about her. Sorry I can't give more information," she said.

"Well, that's better than nothing," Mr. Vanderbilt said.

He was right about that.

"Is there anything else you need?" she asked.

Cheryl had said she knew nothing else about Tasha, so I supposed there was nothing else I needed. I thought of the ripped uniform and wild look I'd seen in Tasha's eyes when she was wrestling with the security guard near my trailer, and I wondered if those eyes were the last thing poor Ellen had seen before she breathed her last.

"No. Thank you for the information, though," I said.

"Not a problem. Good luck. I hope you find out who did it, but Tasha is probably the guilty one. Maybe you're on the right track with that."

"What do you mean by that?"

I had to ask before I let her go.

"Just that they found her stealing, so I wouldn't be surprised if she would murder, too. She probably took that painting."

"Yeah, thanks for the information again," I said.

She turned and headed in the opposite direction. That was odd. I thought she'd been coming to the employees' office. Maybe she had been following me just to find out what I was up to. Nevertheless, I had my information now and was happy about that.

"She seemed convinced that Tasha is the murderer," Mr. Vanderbilt said.

"I suppose Tasha Kenmore would be a likely suspect. But I'm still suspicious of Stan Knowles. Nevertheless, I need to find Tasha and talk to her or find any information about her."

I headed back toward the trailer. Maybe I should have gone in the employees' office and asked other people about Tasha. But that would have been awkward, so I decided I would have to find her address.

"Overall, I'd say that was a successful visit," Mr. Vanderbilt said.

"I'm happy with the info I found," I said. "Now, on to find Tasha."

I pulled out my phone and typed in Tasha's name. When her picture appeared, I recognized her right away. She was the waitress from the restaurant I'd gone to with my family. The one who had been talking to Stan Knowles. They knew each other? Now I was really on to something.

CHAPTER 17

Travel Trailer Tip 17:
You don't have to cut yourself off from the
modern world while in your trailer. Embrace
technology when needed. Wi-Fi works in a
travel trailer, too.

"I tell you, this social media stuff is great. I found her Instagram page, and she made a post today. She works at that restaurant, too," I said, flashing the phone in front of Mr. Vanderbilt's face. "The one I went to with my family. I remember seeing her there."

"Whatever Instagram is," Mr. Vanderbilt said, tossing up his hands. "Sounds like a telegram. The estate wasn't her only job?"

"Apparently not. I wonder if her other employer knows what is going on here."

"Are you going to tell them?" Mr. Vanderbilt asked.

"I don't think I can do that. I just need to go to this restaurant and talk to her."

"Do you think she's working now?"

"We're about to find out," I said. "Let's go."

"I'm ready," Mr. Vanderbilt said, clapping his hands.

There was no sound with his movement. When he talked, I heard him, but I didn't hear his clapping. How odd. Mr. Vanderbilt and I hurried over to my truck and climbed in. Just as I turned the ignition and put the truck into drive, I received a text message. I couldn't stop to check it now. That would have to wait.

"I can't wait to see what happens," Mr. Vanderbilt said. "This truly is a mystery."

The restaurant wasn't far away. Within a short time, we pulled into the parking lot. Over Easy Diner was open twenty-four hours a day, according to the flashing sign in the window. When I turned in, I hadn't expected to see Tasha standing outside talking to Stan Knowles. I suppose I shouldn't have been too surprised.

"This is getting creepy," I said. "Apparently this Stan guy knows everybody."

"That can't be a coincidence," Mr. Vanderbilt said.

"No, it cannot."

I parked the truck. They had no idea I watched them. If only I knew what they were saying. However, I couldn't get out of the car and walk over to them and eavesdrop. Or could I? They had no idea I was watching them, so they probably wouldn't notice if I moved closer. The trouble was that if Stan Knowles saw me, he would recognize me right away. And probably Tasha, too. At this point, did I even care if they recognized me? Possibly not, although if one of them was the killer, that might give them more reason to come after me.

I opened the truck door.

"Where are you going?" Mr. Vanderbilt asked.

"I want to get closer so that I can eavesdrop on them."

"Be careful," Mr. Vanderbilt said as he popped out of the truck.

I quickened my steps across the parking lot, darting behind cars as I went. So far, they hadn't noticed that I was heading their way. I wasn't sure what I would do when I got closer. I couldn't just stand there and stare at them. That would be creepy. I could act as if I were searching for something. Yes, that was what I would do.

When I got closer, I peered at the ground, putting a look of concentration on my face. At least now I would hear their conversation. This would be perfect as long as I wasn't caught. Based on their body stances, waving of arms, and scowls on their faces, I figured they were in a bit of a heated exchange.

"This is scintillating," Mr. Vanderbilt said.

Unfortunately, Stan and Tasha stopped talking now that I had moved closer. Tasha opened the door of the car next to her. Stan watched as she reached inside. A few seconds later, she handed him something, but I couldn't make out what.

"What is this about?" Mr. Vanderbilt asked.

That was what I'd like to know. Stan stepped away from Tasha without another word. She turned and headed back into the restaurant. Mr. Vanderbilt and I watched Stan as he pulled out of the parking lot.

"Now what?" Mr. Vanderbilt asked.

"I guess we'll go into the restaurant," I said.

"I hope you're hungry," he said.

As we walked closer to the restaurant, I noticed the license plate on the car that Tasha had gotten into to retrieve the item for Stan. The plate on the back was personalized with the word SCARY.

"That's interesting." I pointed toward the car.

I hoped no one saw me talking and gesturing. Maybe I should have pretended I was talking on the phone. Otherwise, people would think I was talking to myself.

"What's interesting?" Mr. Vanderbilt asked.

"The license plate has the word 'scary.' I wonder if that's really her car?"

"I wonder if it's a description of her personality? She seemed a bit scary when she was fighting with the security guard."

"Yes, she did seem scary. I'll see what I can find out from her."

"How are you doing that?" he asked.

"I'm going in."

Mr. Vanderbilt and I stepped inside the diner.

The woman at the front door asked, "Table for one?"

I held up two fingers. Oops. I lowered one finger. "Oh, one, yes."

She grabbed a menu and escorted us across the room. Of course, to everyone else, I was alone.

The woman placed the menu on the table. "Enjoy your meal."

Mr. Vanderbilt slid onto the booth across from me. I picked up the menu and pretended to peruse the food options.

"I really hope Tasha will be my waitress. I never thought about that." I talked with my mouth hidden by the menu so that, with any luck, people wouldn't see me talking to myself.

"That would be fortunate," he said.

Scanning the room, I spotted Tasha. So far, she hadn't noticed me, so maybe she really wasn't waiting on my table. Maybe I could question whoever came to help me about her. But that would be difficult. I wasn't even sure how I would ask Tasha questions, much less someone else. It would be an awkward conversation, no matter how I went about it.

"What are you having?" Mr. Vanderbilt asked as he studied the back of the menu. "The desserts are probably divine. That chocolate lava cake . . . oh, my."

"Are you ready to place an order?" The female voice startled me.

Tasha stood beside the table. She hovered a pen above a notepad, waiting for me to speak. Of course, now I was tongue-tied. I suppose I would have to order and wait for her to come back with the food before I could ask questions. If I managed to find my voice.

"I'll have the cheeseburger," I mumbled.

There was no way the burger would be as good as the ones my Aunt Patsy made back in Tennessee. Her burgers were like magic. I thought of Caleb. Aunt Patsy's diner had been the first place we'd gone together. Ever since I took him there, he'd been hooked on my aunt's hamburgers.

"Anything else?" she asked while staring at her order pad.

"That's all," I said.

She grabbed the menu and took off.

"She's not very friendly," Mr. Vanderbilt said.

"Which will make it even harder to ask her questions," I said.

As I waited for the food, I chatted with Mr. Vanderbilt. He told fascinating stories about the estate. His eyes sparkled when he talked about the construction of the mansion, the grand parties that had taken place there, and the large staff that kept it running. Yet oddly, he didn't mention himself in the stories.

I sensed someone watching me. The woman at the table to the left of me was staring. She didn't bother to look away, either. I supposed she wanted me to know she'd been watching. I realized it was because she thought I was talking to myself. Oh well, she'd just have to think I was bonkers.

"That woman was watching you," Mr. Vanderbilt whispered as if she'd overhear him.

"Because I was talking to you. There's nothing I can do about it, though. I can't not talk to you while we sit here."

"You're a sweet person," he said with a smile.

Soon, Tasha returned with the burger. She placed the plate down on the table in front of me.

"Can I get you anything else?" she asked.

At least she acknowledged me this time.

"Can I have ketchup?" I asked.

Okay, that wasn't the question I wanted to ask.

She pointed at the condiment bottle on the table next to me. In a split second, she turned to walk away. I couldn't let her leave without asking something.

"Wait," I called out. "There was one other thing."

When she turned to face me again, I noticed her tight lips and clenched fists right away.

"She's not happy," Mr. Vanderbilt said.

She was unhappy that I had stopped her, but it would be even worse when she realized I was asking odd questions. I couldn't just come out and ask her if she had stolen the painting. I definitely couldn't ask if she had murdered Ellen.

"I think we have a mutual friend," I said with a smile.

"Oh yeah? Who's that?" She placed her hand on her hip.

"Stan Knowles. I've been to his art gallery," I said.

That wasn't a lie. I had been there. Though the fact about him being a friend wasn't true. For all I knew, she wasn't friends with him, either. I had definitely taken a risk by saying that. Tasha stared at me without saying a word. Panic set in. What would I do now?

"You should say something," Mr. Vanderbilt said.

"I saw you talking with Stan when I pulled into the parking lot. I would have said hi, but you all stopped talking before I had a chance. He is your friend, right?"

Did I sound convincing? I wasn't sure. She remained silent. Her behavior was odd, to say the least.

"Try again," Mr. Vanderbilt urged.

"How do you know Stan?" I asked.

"I don't know him well," she said.

At least she had spoken this time.

"Through the art?" I pressed.

"Yes . . . that's it, the art gallery," she said.

"That doesn't sound truthful," Mr. Vanderbilt said.

"I think I've seen you somewhere else before," I said.

"Oh no, Celeste. I know where you're going with this, and I'm not sure it's such a good idea." Mr. Vanderbilt's voice was full of worry. "I don't think you should say it."

Unfortunately, I didn't take his advice.

"Do you also work at the Biltmore? I'm at the arts and crafts fair on the grounds. I thought I saw you around," I said with a smile.

"What do you want?" She raised an eyebrow. "Did they send you here to question me?"

"Uh-oh." Mr. Vanderbilt leaned back in the chair and placed the back of his hand to his forehead as if he might faint.

"Who are they?" I asked. "No one sent me here."

"Oh, now you've made her angry. This is what I was worried about," Mr. Vanderbilt said. "Perhaps you should pay for the meal and leave."

"You know they fired me, and that's why you came here," she said.

Now I had to act surprised by her dismissal.

"I had no idea. I'm sorry that you were fired," I said.

"They got it all wrong. I didn't steal nothin'," she said.

"I believe you," I said, trying to sound sincere. "I imagine it is a stressful time for you."

Mr. Vanderbilt smacked his hand to his forehead once again. "Oh no. I know what you're going to say now, too. For heaven's sake, please stop. I can't handle it."

"Because I was fired?" she asked. "Yes, it is stressful."

"That and the murder at the Biltmore," I said.

Mr. Vanderbilt leaned back again in the seat in a dramatic fashion. "Oh, I can't handle the stress."

The expression on her face instantly changed. She'd seemed angry before, but now she had taken her agitated expression to a whole new scary level.

"You a cop?" she demanded.

"Of course not," I said. "It's just that I figured the murder was on your mind. I know I think about it when I'm there. The idea that the killer could be around is scary."

"The idea that you're possibly talking to the killer right now should be scary for you," Mr. Vanderbilt said. "You should get out of here."

The notion that Tasha might be the killer hadn't been lost on me. I was terrified at the thought. However, I didn't let that stop me.

"Did you know Ellen?" I asked.

"No, I didn't know her," Tasha snapped.

"You never spoke at work? I would think that most of

the tour guides were acquainted with one another, even if just in passing."

"Well, yeah, I saw her, but other than that, I don't think I ever spoke with her."

Interesting. Something didn't add up. I mean, at least she would've said hi to her.

"Were you working at the same time?" I asked.

"I don't know," she said.

It seemed like most of my questions would be met with the same response from her. It was probably pointless to continue asking questions. I would have to change my tactics.

"I'm out of there now, and none of this concerns me," Tasha said.

"What about the fact that Stan Knowles is an art dealer, and a priceless painting was taken from the Biltmore?"

"Are you implying that he took it?" she asked.

"It's possible, no?" I asked.

A middle-aged man in a stained chef's uniform called out to Tasha from behind the counter.

She raised an eyebrow. "Yeah, I bet Stan did it. Now I have to get to work."

Tasha spun around and walked away.

"Her behavior is highly suspicious," Mr. Vanderbilt said.

I took a couple bites of the burger, but I was too anxious to eat. Tasha kept her eye on me while she waited on other tables.

After a few minutes, I put cash on the table. "Let's get out of here."

"I thought you'd never say that." Mr. Vanderbilt jumped up from the table.

I felt Tasha's stare on me as I hurried out of the diner. Bursting out the diner's door, I dashed to my truck and locked the door once inside. A cold chill ran up my spine when I saw Tasha standing at the diner's door, watching me.

"Her stare is chilling," Mr. Vanderbilt said.

I cranked the engine. "That's putting it mildly."

Once out of the parking lot, relief fell over me, but still, I had little information to help me solve this crime. The fact that Stan and Tasha had been talking had to mean something, although she had brushed it off as nothing. However, I thought they were involved in some nefarious activity.

"Be thankful you got out of there safely," Mr. Vanderbilt said. "Although she could come for you. After all, now she knows you're at the craft fair."

"Thanks for making me feel better," I said as I stopped at a red light.

"Just stating the facts. You can't ignore them. If you are aware of the possibilities, you'll be better equipped to deal with them if they actually happen."

I suppose he had a good point.

"I think there's more to her story than she wants to tell," Mr. Vanderbilt said.

"You're right about that, but how will I find out? If only I knew more about her interactions at work. Like through video," I said.

"Whatever that means, yes," he said.

CHAPTER 18

Travel Trailer Tip 18:
Invest in organization storage for your
trailer. It will save you time in the long run.

Another day at the craft fair, and it was once again time to sell my art. Saturday typically was the most lucrative at the fairs, with Sunday a close second. I had everything set out and was trying to focus on the fair instead of a murder investigation. In the past twenty-four hours, I'd sold five paintings. A portrait of Van gazing into the sunset with shades of amethyst and garnet streaking through the candlelight-orange horizon had brought a nice price. I knew others would see his beauty shine from the canvas.

Van was at my feet, resting on his comfy blue-and-white paw-print bed, while Mr. Vanderbilt was roaming around close by. It had been a busy morning, but at the moment, I had a lull in customers. Since it was a bright and sunshiny day, I anticipated a lot of people showing up for the fair this afternoon.

I needed to work on a new painting. That feeling was

creeping into my mind again, and I hoped that something would show up in the images. I caught movement out of the corner of my eye and realized that I had a new customer. But this wasn't a stranger. I recognized her right away. I wondered if there was an ulterior motive for her presence at my booth.

The odd employee was eyeing me as she stepped up to the booth. I had a feeling Cheryl wasn't here for my paintings. What had I done? Was she coming to tell me to mind my own business? She could have told me that when I was asking about Tasha. Something was fishy about this visit.

I pushed to my feet and walked over to her. "Hello, how are you today?"

I was trying to be as friendly as possible.

"I'm just enjoying the beautiful weather and all the crafts," she said with a smile.

Why the turn of attitude? Her personality turned on a dime. I wasn't sure if she was being genuine. Was this all an act? This woman was definitely strange.

"I wanted to check out your lovely artwork," she said.

I wasn't trusting her change of heart. She was up to something. But what? Where was Mr. Vanderbilt? He was intuitive about these things and seemed to be able to read people well. Van stared at her as if waiting for his chance to nibble at her ankles.

"Well, I have quite a few pieces," I said.

"I see that you've been busy," she said.

"I like to stay busy. Whenever the inspiration hits . . . I paint," I said.

She walked around, studying each painting. I remained quiet but watched her movements, wondering when she would reveal her true reason for being there.

"You have lovely paintings, and if I had a great place to hang them, I certainly would buy one."

"Thank you. I appreciate that," I said.

"I'll see you around," she said.

That was it? She was just going to leave without saying anything else? I wasn't sure I believed that. I watched as she walked away, strolling over to another booth selling beaded jewelry.

A slow period settled over the craft fair, and I had no customers, so I decided to continue my painting. Staring at the canvas in front of me, I was happy that I had the wonderful process of artistic creation ahead of me. The most exciting part was when I started something new. Or maybe when I finished. Okay, all of the process was equally exciting.

With my paints beside me, I held the brush in my hand, ready to go. I just had to allow the image to come to mind. I continued swiping the brush against the canvas. After a short time, I finished a painting that depicted the scene of a massive-sized room inside the estate. Mahogany with streaks of spicy brown running throughout the wood covered the walls, and heavy crimson red velvet draperies adorned the windows.

"It's wonderful," Mr. Vanderbilt said.

"Thank you," I said, proud of my work.

"I wonder if there are any other hidden images in there," he said.

"I hope so, but I doubt it. Earlier, I sensed that there would be. I had that feeling, but sadly, that feeling is gone."

After a while, I was satisfied that apparently this was only an image of the inside of a section of the estate— nothing more. Though it was beautiful, I had hoped for more. I just had to hope that I would find another image that gave me a clue.

"This is thrilling," Mr. Vanderbilt said. "Hurry and get the jar again."

The jar was right there, waiting beside me where I'd left it. I picked up the glass and held it to my eye, scanning the canvas for a sign of more skeletons. It only took a couple of seconds until I spotted them. Two were standing outside the window, as if they'd been in front of the estate. They were smaller and harder to see, but I thought they were arguing, too. This time, they were the same size; one wasn't taller than the other. But what did this mean? What kind of clue was this offering me?

Just as with the other skeletons in the painting, these were telling me nothing more than two people had a confrontation. I had expected that. As a matter of fact, it seemed as if a lot of that was going on around the estate. A lot of friction between employees. What was this telling me? That Tasha and Ellen had argued? That was possible, but it was only a guess.

How would I find out for sure? I wished I could get more insight into what was really going on during the work hours at the estate. One way to do that would be to see surveillance videos. But that would be a lot of video, and how would I get access to that in the first place?

"What do you see?" Mr. Vanderbilt asked excitedly.

"Sadly, not much," I said.

"Oh dear, that's disappointing," Mr. Vanderbilt said. "What will you do?"

"I have a plan," I said.

CHAPTER 19

Analyzing the painting I'd just finished, I realized that I should check that specific section in front of the estate. Maybe that was part of the clue. Had Ellen and her killer been at that section at some point? I felt it meant something important that I had painted that particular spot, and the skeletons had showed up outside the window, too.

When the craft fair was over for the day, I packed up my supplies and headed off for that section of the estate. Luckily, Mr. Vanderbilt could tell me exactly where to find it.

"It's just down that way." He pointed.

"Is there any significance to that spot? Do you know what's there?" I asked.

"It's not part of the public tour. I believe they use it for office space," he said.

"Interesting. So the employees would definitely have been there," I said.

"Yes, most definitely," he said.

I couldn't wait to get there. I just hoped that I found someone who was willing to cooperate and possibly give me answers. I stopped just shy of the building when I saw a couple of employees talking. I'd never seen the women before, so at least they wouldn't know me. I wasn't sure what to say, so I darted behind a nearby blood-red rhododendron shrub.

"What are you doing?" Mr. Vanderbilt asked.

"I panicked. I don't know what to say."

"You'd better say something, because you have to find out more about this section of the estate."

"I know, I know. Let me think," I whispered.

"Just be honest. Tell them that you're investigating the murder," Mr. Vanderbilt said.

"Sometimes people don't like that. They won't talk or don't want to be involved. I have to think of something clever," I said.

"Well, I certainly don't know what it would be," Mr. Vanderbilt said.

"I don't either. That's why I'm hiding behind this bush."

"You have a good point," he said.

I peered out at the employees from behind the branches. A few seconds later, the women stopped talking, going separate ways.

"You lost your chance," Mr. Vanderbilt said.

"I know. I messed up."

"What will we do?"

"Maybe I can just go peek in the windows and see what's in there."

"You better hope you don't get caught. They'll kick you out, and you won't be able to sell your paintings."

I knew that was a real possibility, but it was a chance I was willing to take. After a few more seconds, I got up enough nerve to step out from behind the bushes.

"What exactly do you think you're doing?" a male voice asked from over my shoulder.

Spinning around quickly, I almost fell back into the bushes.

"Pierce?" I asked. "Why did you scare me like that?"

"He moves quietly like a cat, doesn't he?" Mr. Vanderbilt said. "How does he do that?"

"What are *you* doing here?" I asked.

"What am I doing here? I think the better question is what are you doing hiding behind the rhododendrons?" Pierce asked.

"That's a valid question. If I answer that, will you answer mine?" I asked.

"Certainly," he said.

I explained what I'd discovered and my thoughts on my findings.

"I thought we were working together." Disappointment lingered in Pierce's words.

"Don't be upset, chap," Mr. Vanderbilt said.

Too bad Pierce couldn't hear Mr. Vanderbilt's words of comfort.

"We were, until you thought I couldn't handle myself," I said.

"I never specifically said that," Pierce said.

"You didn't have to say it," I said.

"I hate to see you two fight. Can't you get along?" Mr. Vanderbilt asked.

"Can you forgive me?" Pierce asked with a pleading gaze.

"How can you say no to that face?" Mr. Vanderbilt pointed.

I couldn't say no to that face.

"All right. Don't do it again, okay?"

"You're back in business." Mr. Vanderbilt clapped his hands.

"I can take care of this. I'll just tell the employee that I'm with the police department and that I need to see the video," Pierce said.

"But that's deceptive," I said.

"Only if they ask. Technically, I am with law enforcement, and I need to see the video," Pierce said.

Mr. Vanderbilt laughed, which of course made me laugh, as well. Pierce laughed, too. Then I sensed someone watching us, which broke up our laughter. Soon, I noticed a random male employee standing by the door. They were everywhere around this place. He stood at attention like a soldier. With his cropped salt-and-pepper hair and broad shoulders, he seemed more like a drill sergeant. Pierce and I must have appeared crazy for standing there, laughing behind the shrubbery.

"This is our chance. I can't wait to talk to him," I said, gesturing with a tilt of my head.

"All right. Let's do this." Pierce stepped out from behind the bush, and I followed him.

With an unpleasant taste in my mouth, and my stomach shaking worse than Grammy's off-balance washing machine, we headed out on our mission. I had to admit it was a bit exciting, although I wasn't sure I could handle this kind of stress all the time. Pierce and Caleb dealt with this on a daily basis.

The employee realized we were walking toward him. His panicked expression told me that he wanted to run away. But since we were staring right at him, he knew he was stuck. So much for this man seeming like a drill sergeant.

"Excuse me, sir," Pierce said.

The man grimaced.

"Yes? The tour starts over there." He pointed.

Pierce pulled out his badge and flashed it at the man. The employee eyed the shiny badge.

"I'm with the police department. We were wondering if this is the area where we would see surveillance video."

"Oh, I'm sorry, we turned over everything to the police already," the man said.

I felt as if my balloon had just been poked.

"What will you do?" Mr. Vanderbilt asked.

I wished I had an answer for that question.

"There may be something we missed," Pierce said.

If we didn't see film from the day of the murder, how would we know what we were searching for? How would we pick a day? We couldn't view months' worth of footage. Did Pierce know what he was doing? I was seriously having doubts.

"Sure, okay," the guy said weakly.

I was just as skeptical as he was.

"What day would you like to see? I have to narrow it down to a time so that I can pull that up for you."

"Does Pierce know what he's doing?" Mr. Vanderbilt asked.

Apparently, we were all questioning Pierce's moves. Did Pierce sense the skepticism from us? When Pierce stared at me, I realized he had no idea what he was doing. And neither did I.

"Somebody had better say something soon," Mr. Vanderbilt said in a singsong voice.

I sifted through a million thoughts in my mind. I had a feeling that the murder hadn't been planned for a super long time, so viewing the day before should be enough.

"We'd like to see the day before, please," I said.

I sure hoped this was the right idea. The chances of us finding anything were slim.

"Do you have a specific time? Or do you want the whole day?" he asked.

"We'd like to see the whole day," I said, trying to sound confident.

"All right. Well, it might take me a bit," he said.

"We have time," I said.

The man headed into the building, leaving me alone with Pierce—and Mr. Vanderbilt, of course.

"Thanks for saving me," Pierce said. "I was a bit frazzled there when he asked. I couldn't think straight."

"It happens to the best of us," Mr. Vanderbilt said as he patted Pierce on the back, but his hand went right through.

Pierce glanced back as if he felt it. I didn't mention that there was a ghost touching him. I didn't want to freak him out even more. He was already flustered from our conversation with the employee.

"We're going to be busy today watching this video," Pierce said.

"Well, I have a little bit of time. Of course, I have to get back to the craft fair. And I assume you do, too. By the way, how are things going?" I asked.

"It's going okay," he said.

He didn't sound that confident. I wondered if that were true.

"Is there anything I can help you with?" I asked.

I wasn't an expert at craft fairs, but I had a couple of them under my belt.

A couple of seconds later, the employee returned. "Here you go."

"That was a lot faster than I thought," Mr. Vanderbilt said.

Pierce took the tiny zip drive from him. "Thank you. We appreciate the help."

"Yes, thank you," I said.

"No problem. Anything I can do to help solve the murder. It's a tragic thing that happened," he said.

"One thing before we leave," Pierce said. "Were you here the day of the murder?"

"I wasn't here that morning, but I have worked with Ellen and saw some things that made me wonder."

"Like what?" I asked.

"Well, she had an argument with Tasha Kenmore recently. Tasha was an employee who worked here."

"I'm familiar with her," I said.

Pierce observed me out of the corner of his eye. I bet he was surprised to know that I had a few details that he may not be privy to. I had a few things up my sleeve, and I was proud of that. Maybe I wasn't such a bad detective, after all.

"They had an argument?" I asked.

I wanted to know all the details.

"Yes, they argued. I wasn't sure what it was about. Just that they definitely were arguing. Their hand gestures, and the way they stormed off, gave it away. I was inside the building, watching out through the window, and saw the squabble. I couldn't hear what was said."

Too bad. If only he had heard what words were exchanged. At least I'd confirmed they had been arguing.

That was a step in the right direction. The fight gave Tasha the motive for murder.

"Do you think she had something to do with Ellen's death?" I asked.

"Tasha?" he asked with a smirk.

The expression on his face let me know that yes, he thought she might be involved.

"It's possible, but I wouldn't want to accuse anyone."

"No, of course not," I said.

"Thank you for the information," Pierce said, shaking the man's hand.

"You're welcome," he said. "I hope you can locate the killer. It's put a black cloud over the Biltmore. People are afraid to be here, thinking that the murderer is still around."

Yes, I could tell by the slow influx of people at the craft fair.

"We're doing our best," I said.

Pierce smiled as we turned to walk away. "You're really good at this. You have a way with people. Getting them to open up and talk when they might not otherwise want to say anything or be involved."

"I guess it's a knack," I said.

"I told you she was good at this," Mr. Vanderbilt said.

"We can get my laptop and check this video." I pointed.

"We might be in for a long night," Pierce said.

"I think he's okay with that," Mr. Vanderbilt said with a smile. "I'd say he was going along with this just to spend time with you. You know you're not going to find anything on that video."

Mr. Vanderbilt had a way of making me blush.

* * *

Pierce and I sat in my trailer with my laptop in front of us. The surveillance video was pulled up on the screen. Pierce sat close to me. Of course, that was the only way, since the place was so tiny, and we both had to see the screen.

"What a cute couple," Mr. Vanderbilt said.

He wasn't helping matters.

"We can skip through the parts where no one is here, right?" I asked.

"Maybe. If we don't find anything on the other hours, we can go back to this. You never know what you might find when people think no one is watching."

"I hadn't thought about that," I said. "But you're right. Do we need snacks for this? Can we fast-forward through it?"

I had a lot of questions.

"Snacks would be good," Pierce said. "I suppose as long as we keep our eyes glued to the screen, we can fast-forward."

"He doesn't sound happy about that," Mr. Vanderbilt said. "I think he wants to watch as slowly as possible to get the maximum time with you."

I ignored Mr. Vanderbilt's comment as I grabbed a bag from the cabinet. "I hope you like pretzels."

"Perfect," Pierce said.

I grabbed a couple of bottles of water from the tiny fridge and sat back down next to Pierce. We watched in silence for a bit as he scanned through, fast-forwarding. Several employees walked back and forth across the camera angle. It was nothing unusual. Until Pierce stopped when we spotted Ellen. She stood in front of the building, checking her watch as if waiting for someone. Only a couple of seconds had passed when Tasha approached.

"Oh, this could be something. It confirms what the drill-sergeant-lookalike employee told us," I said.

Within seconds, the women were in a heated exchange. The employee had been right. This was proof that something was amiss between the two. If only we could figure out what.

"Tasha needs to answer some questions," I said. "I'll have to go back to the diner to speak with her."

"You talked with her?" With an arch of Pierce's right eyebrow, the small scar became more noticeable again.

"That's where she works. I saw her talking with Stan Knowles before I went inside the diner to confront her."

Pierce paused the video. "Wait. You talked to her at the diner?"

"That's right, but I didn't find out much. I have more questions for her, though. She isn't the friendliest, if you know what I mean."

"Yeah, I think I get what you mean. Her behavior doesn't surprise me, since she was fired from the estate. Maybe she can't get along well with others."

When a knock sounded at the door, I almost fell out of my chair.

CHAPTER 20

Travel Trailer Tip 20:
Don't forget to relax and enjoy time with
family, friends, and nature around you. It's
okay to take a break from your murder
investigation now and then.

It wasn't only the knock that had startled me, but Mr. Vanderbilt had screamed. I supposed he was a bit on edge with everything that was going on at the estate.

"Who could that be?" I whispered.

"I'll check for you," Pierce said as he got up from the chair.

I followed him as we moved to the door, which only took a couple of steps. Pierce peeked out the window. A chuckle escaped his lips.

"What's so funny?" I asked.

When he opened the door, I realized why he'd laughed. Caleb seemed surprised, to say the least, to see Pierce open the door.

"Hi, Caleb," I said.

Why did I feel guilty as if I'd done something wrong? Caleb remained speechless for several seconds.

"I was just stopping by to check on you. Now I see you are doing well." Caleb eyed Pierce.

"We were just reviewing surveillance video," I said.

Caleb shoved his hands into his jeans pockets. "Did you find anything?"

"We did," I said excitedly. "Tasha Kenmore and Ellen were fighting the day before her murder."

He scrunched up his face, as if he had no clue who I was talking about.

"Tasha was an employee here who was fired for stealing. Maybe Ellen confronted her about stealing, and Tasha had to get rid of her."

"It's a very good theory," Caleb said. "Did you speak with anyone about this?"

"The other day I spoke with Tasha, but that was before I had this information. Now I'm going back."

Caleb stared at Pierce. "I suppose you're going with her."

"The thought has crossed my mind, yes," Pierce said.

"Well, let me know if you need any help," Caleb said.

I knew Caleb wasn't all right with this. Maybe when I found the killer, he would realize that it had been for the best.

"Thank you," I said.

"I'll let you all get back to whatever you were doing," Caleb said. "I have a few things I need to catch up on."

I wanted to say more, but the words didn't come. Caleb turned and walked away.

"Bye, Caleb," I called out.

He tossed his hand up over his shoulder. Now I had a sinking feeling in the pit of my stomach.

"That was sad," Mr. Vanderbilt said.

Yes, it was sad. Tears formed in my eyes, but I had to hold it together in front of Pierce.

"I suppose it's getting late," I said. "Maybe we can go tomorrow to the diner."

"Sounds like a plan," Pierce said. "I'll meet you here at your trailer after the fair is over."

"Okay, that sounds good," I said.

Pierce stepped out of the trailer. He turned to face me before leaving. "You'll call me if you need anything, right?"

"Absolutely," I said with a smile.

He studied my face for a bit longer before turning to walk away. "I'll see you tomorrow, Celeste."

A rustling noise made me spin around. I'd thought for sure someone was walking up behind me. No one was around, but my heart had certainly gotten a jolt. Not to mention it felt as if someone were watching me. Perhaps they were hidden by the night or lurking behind a nearby tree.

"Is anyone out there?" I called out.

No one answered, but I hadn't expected a response. I wouldn't search for the person, either. I was brave, but not stupid. Of course, I was on edge, so maybe my mind was making something out of nothing. It could have just been the wind. A breeze carried across my skin with a delicate touch. Yes, it had to have been the wind. So why did I still have an uneasy feeling?

After crawling under the covers, I attempted to fall asleep, but slumber eluded me. I felt a presence in the room with me. Mr. Vanderbilt stood by the window.

"Did I wake you?" he asked.

"I'm awake," I said.

Mr. Vanderbilt slumped his shoulders.

"Is something on your mind?" I sat up in bed.

"Nothing, I suppose," he said.

Based on his posture, I suspected he wasn't being honest.

"Mr. Vanderbilt, I've been meaning to ask, but things have been so hectic. Do you remember anything from your personal past yet? You told stories of the estate, but nothing about yourself. I thought some things might be coming back to you by now."

He released a sigh. "You're right. I remember things about the estate, but not about myself. It's not for a lack of trying."

"I hope it comes to you soon," I said. "Maybe if you don't think about it so much, it'll pop into your head. If you think about it too hard, it'll stop the flow in your mind."

Did that make sense? I was kind of winging it with this advice. Just because I painted ghosts to this spiritual plane didn't mean I had a clue about the paranormal world.

"I appreciate you thinking of me," he said.

"That's what friends are for," I said.

"I like that saying. That's a good one," he said.

"I'm not the one who thought of it first," I said around a yawn.

"I should let you get back to sleep," he said.

I scooted back down on the bed and pulled the cover up to my chin. Van snuggled up next to me again, relieved that the talking was over. Every few seconds, Mr. Vanderbilt sighed. That was my signal that he obviously wasn't finished with the conversation.

"Oh, I just thought of something," Mr. Vanderbilt said.

His voice boomed across the tiny trailer. He had probably talked much louder than he had anticipated. Van and I, of course, had been startled by his loud outburst.

"What did you think of? You'd better tell me fast before I get woozy from nerves," I said.

"It's a name," he said.

"What's the name?" I asked.

"Nathaniel Nally," he said matter-of-factly.

"Do you know Nathaniel Nally?"

He hesitated before continuing, "It keeps coming to my mind that I am Nathaniel Nally."

"I don't understand," I said.

"Neither do I," he said.

"You're Mr. Vanderbilt."

"Yes, I suppose I am," he said.

I felt bad for him, because he didn't remember any of his past. I wished there were something more I could do.

"If you remember any more details, please let me know, so I can try to figure it out."

"I'll be sure to let you know if I think of anything else," he said.

I picked up my phone and searched for the name Nathaniel Nally. Nothing came up. While I was looking, I pulled up Mr. Vanderbilt's photo again. Now that I thought about it, there were differences in the features. I thought maybe I'd just been a bit off my game when I'd painted the portrait. The man standing in my trailer was definitely the man on the canvas, but now I wasn't convinced he was William Vanderbilt.

I'd closed my eyes, hoping to fall asleep, but still nothing. After a few seconds, I opened my eyes. Mr. Vanderbilt was no longer in the trailer. I suppose he'd left me to sleep. Something was bothering me, though, and I knew I wouldn't sleep until I finished. Yes, the urge to paint had taken over. It hit at all times of the day. There was no sense in ignoring it.

I needed to do one more painting before the craft fair was over. Climbing out of bed, I pulled out my paints, set up a canvas, and immediately got to work. Soon, a beautiful woman was on the canvas. She had long golden hair that tumbled past her shoulders. She wore a white dress embroidered with lace. The high collar and full, puffy sleeves led me to believe that the portrait was from the early 1900s. I had no idea who she was, but her crystal-blue eyes stared back at me as if she wanted me to find answers. Anxiety took over as I wondered if she would turn up as a ghost, as well. After finishing, I studied the portrait. When nothing more came to me, I turned the canvas around and climbed back into bed. I didn't want the woman staring at me all night.

I had a hard time going to sleep. When the sun popped up, streaming through the tiny openings in the blinds of my trailer, I groaned and pulled the covers over my head. A voice in my mind reminded me that I had customers arriving soon, and I needed to get to work. All I wanted to do was stay in bed, but there was so much to be done that I wouldn't have the luxury of a lazy morning. Not only was there work to be done with the paintings, but with finding the killer. I groaned again and tossed the covers off my legs.

Van popped up from under the covers, ready to start the day. He wagged his tail as usual. He was the happiest dog I'd ever seen. Even when stuck in a cage at the animal shelter, he had been like a ray of sunshine. We were there for each other. I helped him, and he helped me. Not to mention, he was a good sleuthing partner. He had a nose for finding the clues.

I climbed out of bed. "Okay, Van, we have to get this day going."

As I headed over to the kitchen to grab his food, Van scampered along behind me. He sat in front of the dish, patiently waiting. Once he was fed, it was time for me to scavenge for nourishment. I supposed it would be cereal again. A reminder of Aunt Patsy's diner flashed in my mind. What I wouldn't do for a stack of her pancakes. The maple syrup dripped down the sides of the fluffy stack. The buttery taste rushed back to me.

Not only were the pancakes great, but the French toast and Danishes, too. Perhaps it was a good thing that I wasn't there. I'd stick with my sensible breakfast. A vision of an omelet popped into my head. I'd better eat my cold cereal before I got carried away with memories. I'd have to call Aunt Patsy later and check in. It had been a while, and I missed her.

I'd just finished the last bite of corn flakes when inspiration hit. I hurried and got my supplies ready. Van watched as I scurried around the trailer. I set my canvas on the easel and got out the paints. I'd have to hurry, because I didn't want to be late getting my paintings out on display. That would appear unprofessional.

What would I discover in the painting this time? I was so excited that I could barely pick up the brush. Van stared up at the blank canvas. His presence reminded me that Mr. Vanderbilt was nowhere around. I hadn't seen him this morning. He was always so excited for a new painting. I scanned the tiny space to see if he was standing in the corner. He was nowhere in sight. I supposed he would pop up soon enough, but right now, I had to get to work. I dipped the brush into the paint.

A blue sky with fluffy clouds formed as my brush moved

across the canvas. Next, I found myself dipping into the pink paint. It didn't take long until I realized I was painting my pink trailer. Oh, how fun. This would be a great portrait to keep inside the trailer, a fun addition to my decor. I even added the string lights and the lawn chairs out front, with Van sitting beside the door. Why hadn't I painted this before?

I was excited to see if the scene held a hidden image. Since the painting was done, it was time to grab my jar. I might have set a time record with painting this one. I'd seen the trailer so many times that getting it just right was easy. I quickly picked up the glass so that I could check for an image. Only five minutes to get the paintings out before people arrived.

I put the glass up to my eye, scanning the painting for anything out of the ordinary. I moved up and down and all around, but so far, I hadn't spotted a hidden image. This was a bummer. What if I found nothing? I was ready to give up when I saw it. I almost dropped the glass. The air felt like it had been sucked from my lungs.

Hidden from the naked eye were two skeletons. One was strangling the other. They were right in front of my trailer. I knew what this meant. One of the skeletons was a portrayal of me. The other was the killer. This was a warning. I had no idea what to do. When would this happen? Was someone waiting to attack me as soon as I stepped out of the trailer? Could I avoid this? I couldn't stay in here forever. I checked my watch. As a matter of fact, I had to go out now. I set the glass down. I didn't want to see this any longer.

Muffled voices came from outside my trailer. Midway to the door, I stopped in my tracks.

CHAPTER 21

Travel Trailer Tip 21:
You might want to pack something to use as a
weapon in your trailer. In case you have to
go into survival mode.

Van's ears perked up, letting me know that he heard voices, too. Someone was right outside the trailer. They were having a conversation. Two men, perhaps? Was it Caleb and Pierce? I peeked out the tiny window on the door but saw no one. I supposed I had to go out and check, even though my anxiety was through the roof. After seeing that image, I would be in constant fear.

I inhaled a gulp of air and released it before turning the doorknob and inching the door open. People around me were setting up their items for the day, but I saw no one around my trailer.

"Van, you stay here. I'll be right back," I said.

I inched out the trailer and closed the door behind me. Pushing back what felt like the onset of a panic attack, I reached the bottom step. I eased around the side of the trailer. When I bumped into a tall, muscular man, I screamed.

"What is the matter with you?" Stevie asked.

"What's the matter with *me*? What's the matter with *you*? What are you doing?"

Stevie and Hank were at the back of the trailer.

"We're checking out our handiwork here." Stevie pointed at the addition on the back of my trailer.

"Surprisingly, it's still there," I said. "You all nearly scared me to death."

"Why are you so on edge?" Hank asked.

It wasn't like I could explain what I'd just seen in the hidden image. They would just laugh at me, as usual. They never took anything like that seriously.

"Well, when I hear strange voices outside and there's been a murder, I get a little antsy, excuse me."

"Typical sassy attitude," Stevie said. "She's just like Mom."

"I heard that," my mother said as she walked around the corner of the trailer.

My dad and grandmother were close behind.

"Well, the gang's all here," I said.

"Of course, we're here. We came to help," my mother said.

Oh no, this was not the help I needed right now. But I supposed I could use some help putting up the paintings, considering I had one minute left until the show opened for the day.

"Grab the paintings and set them out if you want to help me."

"You heard her, everybody, get to work," my dad said.

They all grabbed paintings and put them out. I was glad they were here, because I felt a little better about what I'd seen. But they wouldn't be here forever. At least I hoped not. Once they were gone, I would be back to worrying about the killer lurking around, ready to attack.

"How is it?" my mother asked.

"Well, I'm not sure how Stevie and Hank got on top of the roof of the trailer to put paintings up there, but it's probably better that we take them down." I pointed. "If someone wants to buy one, I won't be able to get it."

"What is going on here?" a woman asked from over my shoulder.

I spun around and saw Sammie standing behind me.

"Oh, my gosh," I yelled, reaching out and hugging her. "When did you get here?"

"I just rolled into town and came straight here," she said. "I haven't even had a chance to get my morning coffee."

"Well, we'll have to solve that problem," I said.

"What is going on around here?" Sammie asked again. I knew she was surprised to see my entire family.

"My family is helping set up the paintings. And as you can see, in typical fashion, my brothers went above and beyond." I gestured with my arm toward the chaotic scene.

Sammie laughed. "Well, I guess you can say at least they're helping."

"I guess I could say that," I said.

"No worries. I'm here to help to you now. And we're going to rock this craft fair." Sammie lowered her voice. "Did they find out anything about the murder?"

"The police haven't found out much that I know of," I said. "But never fear, I'm on the case."

"Oh no. You didn't tell me you were snooping around playing detective," she said.

"I just figured you assumed."

"Well, I should have assumed, I guess. I worry about you, Celeste. I don't want you to get hurt."

"That's what Caleb said. And Pierce, until he relented and is now helping me."

"Pierce and you are working together?" She raised an eyebrow.

"Yeah, I suppose we are. Neither Caleb nor Pierce is officially a detective on the case. I suppose Pierce feels like he can help me because of that."

"Have you found anything?" she asked.

"A few things."

I pulled out a painting of an autumn sunset with golden beams of sun spilling light over pops of jade, tangerine, and burgundy leaves. I set it up while I filled her in on all that I had recently discovered. I contemplated whether I should tell her about the hidden image I'd just seen. It was bothering me, and I felt like I should tell someone. But telling her would only upset her. And I didn't want that, so for the time being, I would just keep it to myself. I also hated that I felt I was putting everyone around me in danger. Just by being near me, they could be at risk. Or maybe by being around people, I would keep the killer away from me.

The first customer approached my booth—a lanky man with long gray hair and a cane. Right away, my brothers tried to talk the man into a painting. I had to get them out of here before they chased everyone away with their aggressive sales pitch. I liked to let the paintings speak for themselves. If the person was drawn to one, they would buy it; no need to convince them. I felt like I would have happier customers that way.

I rushed over and stepped in front of my brothers. "Let us know if you need any more help."

"Thank you," the man said, not taking his eyes off Hank and Stevie.

I grabbed their arms and pulled them to the side. "Stop doing that."

"Doing what?" Stevie asked innocently.

"Scaring away the customers," I whispered.

My mother directed my brothers away from the area. They listened only to her. They knew not to make Mama mad.

"Your brothers are a handful," Sammie said.

"I try to forget. Listen, there's a food truck nearby." I pointed. "Why don't you go get some coffee?"

"How about I stay here? You take a break and get me some coffee? I think you might need to get away for a minute."

My brothers were play-fighting and throwing punches at each other. "You know, that might be a good idea. Okay, coffee coming up. Is there anything else you would like?"

"Do they have doughnuts?" she asked. Sammie was an excellent baker herself, but she also enjoyed the down-to-earth sweetness of a store-bought doughnut.

"I do believe so."

"Okay, one doughnut." She held up her index finger. "But only one. I'm watching my figure." She placed her hands on her slim hips.

"Two doughnuts coming up," I said.

She glared at me.

"One for me," I said with a wink.

"Oh, all right, that's fine," she said.

After collecting orders for my mom, dad, grandma, and brothers, I headed out toward the food truck.

Sammie's Strawberry Rhubarb Pie

Prep time: 50 minutes; Cook time: 65 minutes

Ingredients:
1 large egg
4 to 5 tablespoons ice water, divided
¾ teaspoon white vinegar
2¼ cups all-purpose flour
¾ teaspoon salt
¾ cup cold lard

For the filling:
1¼ cups sugar
6 tablespoons quick-cooking tapioca
3 cups sliced fresh or frozen rhubarb, thawed
3 cups halved fresh strawberries
3 tablespoons butter
1 tablespoon 2 percent milk
Coarse sugar

In a small bowl, whisk egg, 4 tablespoons ice water, and vinegar until blended.

In a large bowl, mix flour and salt; cut in lard until crumbly.

Gradually add egg mixture, tossing with a fork, until dough holds together when pressed. If mixture is too dry, slowly add additional ice water, a teaspoon at a time, just until mixture comes together.

Divide dough in half. Shape each into a disk; wrap in plastic. Refrigerate 1 hour or overnight.

Preheat oven to 400 degrees.

In a large bowl, mix sugar and tapioca. Add rhubarb and strawberries; toss to coat evenly. Let stand fifteen minutes.

On a lightly floured surface, roll one half of dough to a $\frac{1}{8}$-inch-thick circle and then transfer to a 9-inch pie plate.

Trim pastry even with rim. Add filling and dot with butter. Roll remaining dough to a 1/8-inch-thick circle. Place over filling. Trim, seal, and flute edge. Cut slits in top. Brush milk over pastry; sprinkle with coarse sugar.

Bake for twenty minutes. Reduce oven setting to 350 degrees and bake 45–55 minutes or until crust is golden brown and filling is bubbly.

Cool pie on a wire rack.

CHAPTER 22

Travel Trailer Tip 22:
Use sage to keep mosquitoes away. This
probably won't work on a killer, though.

Leaves tumbled toward the ground as I walked along the tranquil path. Halfway to the food truck, an idea hit me. Yes, I got a bit sidetracked easily. This was important, though, and I was sure everyone would understand if their coffees were a bit delayed. Okay, maybe my brothers wouldn't be so understanding.

I headed for the estate. Crowds of people moved around the beautiful grounds. I wanted to view the crime scene one more time. Honestly, I didn't want to see the spot again, but I felt as if this were something I had to do. The area had been opened back up to the public for tours, and it was business as usual. Maybe I was crazy to even think about going back in there to the scene of the crime. I should just put all of this out of my mind. I was in too deep now, though.

Had the police missed something? Yeah, that was unlikely, but the overwhelming feeling of checking it out made me head right into the mansion. Everyone would wonder what happened to me if it took too long in there, so I would have to hurry. The last thing I needed was my family calling for a search party or reporting me missing. It wouldn't be the first time they'd done that. A couple of years ago, I spent a little too long in Target and forgot my phone in the car. By the time I checked out, my mother had already called private investigators to help find me.

I declined going with a tour group. Even though I had access to the estate grounds for the craft fair, I didn't have unlimited tour admissions. We'd been allowed one free tour. Anything further and I'd have to purchase a ticket. I just wanted to go out on my own. No need to see the whole mansion. Nervousness hit me as I stepped inside the hallway leading to the room where I'd found Ellen's body. It looked calm and orderly, as if there had never been a murder. What had I expected? To still see the chalk outline of her body? Crime-scene tape still draped across the room? Sounds echoed through the massive, tall-ceilinged chamber. Giant portraits, vases, and other expensive items decorated the space. Thick velvet drapes hung from the windows.

Stepping across the marble floor, I came to the room where I'd found Ellen just a few days ago. In one way, it seemed like minutes, and in another, it seemed like years. I stared from the doorway, peering over the area. I suppose standing over here wouldn't do much good. I had to get closer for a better view. My stomach twisted into an even tighter knot at the thought. Nevertheless, I had to do this.

I stepped over to the spot where I had found the body. Did the people who were currently taking a tour even know what had happened here? A new tour guide had taken over the area. If I worked here, I would be nervous that the killer could return. What if the person was targeting tour guides? That theory couldn't totally be ruled out. Though why they would focus on tour guides was beyond me. Just another part of the mystery.

As I stood there surveying the room, I sensed someone behind me. Spinning around, I took in the entire room, but no one in the nearby group of tour-goers seemed interested in me. Perhaps Mr. Vanderbilt was hiding from me. Yes, that had to be it. It was odd that he hadn't made an appearance all morning. Not even when my family arrived. They might be the reason he stayed away, though. I wouldn't blame him. Nevertheless, I assumed I was just sensing his presence.

This was silly. Why was I here? The police had checked the scene. There was nothing left for me to find. I decided it was time for me to get out of there. Coffee and doughnuts were calling my name.

As I took in one last scan of the surroundings, something shiny on the floor caught my attention. Hidden behind an ornate buffet-style table was a gold object. I checked to see if anyone was watching me. If the tour guide spotted me fishing around on the floor, he would call security. Luck was on my side, since he was distracted by a middle-aged man wearing a bright orange Hawaiian shirt. Had he gotten on the wrong plane? Instead of Honolulu, he'd ended up in North Carolina. Bless his heart; at least he was keeping the tour guide busy. I just needed him to stay distracted for a couple more minutes. Just long enough for me to grab the sparkly object.

I inched over to the table, trying to act nonchalant. In

reality, I was probably being completely obvious. Luckily, no one noticed my movements. I stood with my back against the table now. I was able to get close and eased down to the floor, stretching my arm back. I fumbled around on the floor, trying to make contact with the item. Where was the thing? Finding it without taking my eyes off the tour guide was tough. My fingers touched something cold. Aha. I'd made contact. Now I hoped the thing didn't slip through my fingers.

I stretched my arm out from under the table with my hand firmly clutching the object. My hand shook after my stealth mission. With the tour guide still distracted, I opened my fist to see what treasure I'd unearthed. A shiny gold keychain. It was the shape of a heart and had a single gold key attached.

The initials S.K. were etched on the front. Well, this couldn't be Ellen's. With the amount of people that came through here on a daily basis, this keychain could belong to anyone. So why was I thinking it might have something to do with the murder? Because it couldn't be ruled out that the killer had dropped this when they'd been in the act?

It was probably nothing to do with that, but I would keep it in my mind. Besides, how would I find out who owned the keychain and what the key was for? That was like finding a needle in a haystack. A thought popped into my head. S.K. Stan Knowles? He was on my suspect list. It was probably a crazy thought. Nevertheless, I had to consider the possibility.

The man in the Hawaiian shirt walked away, and the tour guide's attention turned to me. Our eyes met, and I stood frozen. Guilt had to be written on my face.

"May I help you?" he asked with a note of aggravation in his voice.

It was time for me to get out of there.

"No, thank you. I was just taking in the beauty of the room," I said with a nervous laugh.

He watched me as I hurried across the room. Glancing over my shoulder as I rushed out the door, I saw that he remained focused on me. I hoped he wouldn't call security. Did he recognize me as the woman who had found Ellen's body? I burst out of the estate and into the fresh sunshine. Thank goodness I'd escaped. The keychain was still in my hand. There was no way I would let it go.

An adrenaline rush hit me as I hurried toward the food stand. Just a bit of a lead had set off the excitement in me. I doubted it would come to anything, but I was proud that I had discovered something else. As I stood in line at the food truck, I studied the keychain. Yes, this could definitely belong to Stan Knowles. It could have fallen from his pocket in the struggle with Ellen.

I was heading back to my trailer, trying to balance all of the items in my arms, when I heard the sound of footsteps. They crunched against ground with a distinct sound. I felt as if I were being followed. I quickened my steps while trying to keep the coffee from spilling. Sucking in a few gulps of air, I felt fear flutter in my chest. I couldn't walk any faster without dropping everything. Maybe I should just toss the food and coffee on the ground and run for my life. Or I could turn around and confront the person behind me. No—what if it was the killer? That would be a bad idea. I needed to get out of here.

Other people around didn't seem to notice me, or anything unusual. Maybe it was just my mind playing tricks on me. I was being paranoid. It was easy for that to happen with the fear of a killer being around. Why couldn't Caleb or Pierce show up right about now?

Sammie ran over when she saw me with armfuls of drinks and food. She grabbed the coffees from my hands. The expression on my face told her that I had been in some kind of scary situation. She knew me well.

"Where have you been?" she asked. "You had me worried to death. I was ready to call the police."

"Oh, you know, here and there," I said, taking a bite out of a doughnut.

"I'm not buying that."

I pointed at my mouth as if to say it was full and I couldn't possibly answer.

"I can wait," she said, crossing her arms in front of her.

When I finished chewing, I said, "Well, I guess you're wondering what happened to me."

"Obviously," she said.

"I found this keychain, and I just think that there's something important about it." I pulled the keychain from my pocket. "It was in the area where I found Ellen."

"I just don't want you to get in trouble," she said.

"No trouble here," I said. "There is somewhere else I need to go. Would you be able to watch the booth for me?"

"Of course, that's what I'm here for, to help. But this place you're going, will it get you in trouble?" Sammie asked.

"No, of course not," I said with a smile.

My brothers and dad had devoured their breakfast snacks in seconds. My mother and grandmother were daintily nibbling theirs.

"Slow down. Eating that fast is bad for your digestive system," my mother warned.

She said that on a daily basis, but they never listened. My mother managed to get them to the car and headed to the hotel. I knew that my dad had work to do, as well. He might be surrounded by chaos, but he was focused on work. I took after him regarding that, but not so much on the clumsiness, much to my mother's happiness. I was more like her in that respect.

Sammie and I watched as my family drove away.

"I feel like we just weathered a storm," I said.

She laughed. "But they're great, and they love you."

"Yeah, I suppose they are crazy, but great. I'm lucky to have them."

"Just remember you said that the next time they're wreaking havoc in your life."

After leaving Sammie at the booth, I drove to the diner. I parked the truck and got out. When I spotted a couple of employees standing outside, I became interested in what they might be discussing. A man and a woman were in earnest conversation.

"What are you doing?" a male voice asked from over my shoulder.

I jumped and spun around. "Oh, you scared me," I said, seeing nobody there.

"Oops," he said.

I clutched my chest. "Where have you been, Mr. Vanderbilt?"

"I was hiding out from your family. I didn't want them to see me."

"They can't see you," I said.

Still, Sammie had seen the other ghost. Maybe she would be able to see him, too.

"Are you sure?" he asked.

"Positive. Even if my friend and family saw you, they'd be fine with that. You're nice. There's no reason to be scared. They're a little crazy but otherwise harmless."

The ghost was afraid of my family? How ironic was that?

"If you say so," he said. "That brings me back to the question, what are you doing here?"

"I'm listening in on their conversation. At least, I was trying to."

"What are they saying?" he asked. "You need to be careful."

"Give me just a minute, and I'll explain." I turned my attention back to the dark-haired man and woman.

The vanilla-malt blonde crossed her arms in front of her apron-covered waist. She wore the bluebell-covered uniform dress. He wiped his hands on his black pants. Apparently, he'd lost his apron somewhere along the way.

"What's going on here?" a female voice asked from over my shoulder.

I jumped again. Mr. Vanderbilt flinched, as well.

"Oh, my goodness, Grammy. What are you doing here?" I asked. "You nearly scared me to death."

"I thought you were acting strange, so I decided to take your mother's car and come check on you."

"You took mom's car?"

"She didn't say I couldn't."

"I'm pretty sure she wouldn't want you to take it. And

I'm not sure how you can even see over the steering wheel."

My grandmother was a petite woman and sat on pillows to see out of the car. I supposed what my grandmother always said was true: where there was a will, there was a way.

"Don't you worry about me. I get things done if they need to be done," she said.

"I don't doubt that, Grammy."

"So what's going on here? Why are you acting so suspicious?" she asked.

"I'm not acting suspicious," I said.

She raised an eyebrow. "Now tell Grammy the truth."

"You always know the truth, don't you, Grammy?"

"Always," she said.

"I'm spying on that man and woman over there."

"Well, get back to it," she said.

The three of us turned and stared at the couple. Of course, Grammy didn't know that there was a third person with us.

Grammy nudged me. "What are you doing standing back here? You should go over there and listen to them. At the least, you'll hear better."

"Even better, maybe you should talk to them," Mr. Vanderbilt said.

"Is everything all right, dear?"

My grandmother had no idea that the ghost was talking to me. Should I tell her about Mr. Vanderbilt? Could I really do what Mr. Vanderbilt suggested? How would I start a conversation with them?

"I was just thinking that maybe I should go over and talk to those people. What will two strangers think when I ask about another stranger?"

"I'd ask for directions, that always works," she said.

"I want to ask about another woman who works here," I said.

"Well, it certainly can't hurt to start a conversation," my grandmother said. "It's better than hiding over here by this car and trying to eavesdrop."

At this point, the people hadn't noticed me.

"I guess I can give it a shot, but I don't know how to start a conversation."

"Ask about the food here," Grammy said.

"I like the way you think, Grammy," I said. "That's a great idea."

"Now I see where you get your smarts from," Mr. Vanderbilt said.

I should tell Grammy about that compliment. She loved compliments. I thought she'd like Mr. Vanderbilt, too. Pushing my shoulders back, I headed over toward the man and woman. They watched me, obviously curious as to my intentions.

When I approached, I said, "I hate to bother you, but I was wondering if you can tell me . . ."

Now I probably appeared terrified. I had no idea what to ask for. My mind had gone blank under the pressure.

"The nearest post office," I blurted out. "I nearly forgot I need to mail a letter today."

They stared at me as if I'd asked for the nearest train to the moon.

"Well, they're not the friendliest bunch, are they?" Mr. Vanderbilt asked.

"I think there's one just down the street," the woman said. A crease formed between her barely visible blonde eyebrows as she pointed.

At least she was talking to me. That was definitely a start. But how would I transition the conversation now?

"Great. Thanks. I'll have to head there right after I have breakfast. Is the food good here?" I asked.

I was running out of ideas on what to talk about. And I was beginning to get even stranger stares from the employees.

"I recognize that little red Mazda from the Biltmore Estate." I pointed.

I acted as if this were a random sighting. They didn't need to know that this was all planned. It was all in the name of solving a crime. Where they on to me? How would I explain my question? I was just being a little too nervous.

"Do you know Tasha?" I asked.

"Yeah, we work with her," the guy said as he tossed a cigarette butt onto the ground.

I wanted to go over and pick it up or make him pick it up. No need to litter when there was a trash can nearby. Didn't he want to keep the parking lot nice and pretty? Having litter around certainly wouldn't accomplish that. But the litterbug was the least of my worries right now. I needed to focus.

"Yeah, we know her," the woman said.

"Oh, really? That's great. I know she was a hard worker at the estate."

The woman laughed. "Things must have changed, because she sure isn't doing that here."

"Oh, this doesn't sound good," Mr. Vanderbilt said.

"Really? I'm sorry to hear that," I said. "Maybe she's going through a stressful time right now."

Where did I even come up with the stuff? The words just slipped from my mouth without a second thought.

"Yeah, I suppose that could be it. She has been acting weird lately," the woman said.

"How so?" I asked.

They probably thought it was strange that I was discussing this with them. I really didn't have a reason for asking the questions. Maybe they thought I was just being a gossip.

A car pulled into the parking lot. When the man got out, I recognized the driver. Stan Knowles.

"Oh, speaking of weird," the woman said as she watched Stan.

"He really has been here a lot," I said.

I regretted saying that once it had slipped out. They'd wonder how I knew Stan had been here a lot.

"Do you know him?" I asked.

"Actually, I do. Well, I just know of him," the woman said.

"Is Tasha friends with him?" I pressed.

"I don't know what their status is," the woman said.

"Really? That's interesting. Maybe that's why she's been distracted at work," I said.

"I think something's going on with them," the man said.

It sounded as if something was going on, and I wanted to get to the bottom of it. Stan walked into the diner. Now, more than ever, I wanted to get inside.

"Oh, now you have to go inside and eat," Mr. Vanderbilt said.

I thought Mr. Vanderbilt and Grammy liked this diner, too.

CHAPTER 23

Travel Trailer Tip 23:
A trailer can be just as comfortable as home.
Add personal touches like photos and toss
pillows. Keep your trailer neat so you will be
prepared for visitors, including ghosts.

My grandmother must have been on the same wavelength, because she said, "We should go inside and eat now, dear."

"Oh, right," I said with a smile. "I almost forgot."

I knew that the couple had suspicions about me, but it didn't matter at this point. As long as I didn't continue my suspicious behavior, they'd probably forget all about me. I looped my arm to my grandmother's, and we marched for the diner. Mr. Vanderbilt followed behind, rushing around and grabbing at the door handle as if he were going to open the door for us. Oh, how sweet was that. Unfortunately, his hand went right through. It was the thought that counted, though.

I thought maybe Mr. Vanderbilt had a bit of a crush on

my grandmother. How would I tell her that a ghost had taken a fancy to her? Perhaps I would just keep that information to myself. I opened the door and allowed my grandmother to walk through. As soon as I stepped into the diner, the smell of cheeseburgers and french fries hit me.

Mr. Vanderbilt walked ahead. He seemed mesmerized by the glass display case full of baked goods.

He pointed. "Oh, you simply have to get a slice of this chocolate cake."

Maybe I would get a slice, and that would make Mr. Vanderbilt happy. I scanned the area for Stan Knowles or Tasha. After a few seconds, I spotted Stan, sitting at a booth in the corner of the room. Next, I scanned the space for Tasha. Seconds later, I found her behind the counter. She was waving her arms and pointing as she argued with another employee. That didn't surprise me much.

Was Stan seated in her section? I wanted to get close so that I could eavesdrop on their conversation. Lucky for me, the booth right behind him was empty. I didn't wait for anyone to tell me where to sit.

"The booth in the back, Grammy," I said.

With my grandmother beside me, we marched toward the table. We were on a mission. Stan stared at the menu as we slid into the booth. I sat directly behind Stan so he wouldn't notice me. Plus, I would have an easier time hearing any conversation if and when Tasha came over. My grandmother could be the eyes for me and tell me about their body language with each other. I was anxious and excited about what I might discover. My grandmother and I picked up menus. Mr. Vanderbilt was still standing in front of the glass display case. He was transfixed by the baked goods.

"Nothing's going on at the moment," Grammy said. "I think he just took a drink of water."

"You don't have to tell me every detail, Grammy," I whispered.

She winked. "Right. Gotcha."

Mr. Vanderbilt came unglued from the display case and came over. "I can sit at the table with him and listen in on the entire conversation."

How would I answer him? I nodded. Luckily, he understood and left the table. I glanced over my shoulder to see where he'd gone.

"Oh, don't do that, dear," Grammy said.

I smiled. "Right. I forgot."

"It's okay, we're just learning how to do this," she said.

A couple of seconds later, I spotted Tasha out of the corner of my eye. She was headed toward Stan's table. My anxiety spiked. This was the moment when we might really discover something. They probably wouldn't say too much for fear of a stranger overhearing them. I wondered if Tasha would recognize me. Maybe I should have just sent Grammy in here alone. No, I had to do this. That was the only way I would feel confident that I had all the info.

"I didn't expect to see you here so soon," Tasha said when she approached Stan's table.

My grandma and I both stared at each other.

"You didn't return my calls," he said. "I had no choice but to come over here. Deidre didn't bring me the painting, so I took matters into my own hands. I expect you to keep up your end of the bargain, too."

Oh, this was getting juicy. My anxiety increased even more.

"I didn't think there was anything left to say," Tasha said.

"The police have been coming around," he said.

Oh my gosh, they were talking a lot more than I'd thought they would.

"Yeah, I know that," she said. "They talked to me, too."

"What did you tell them?" he asked.

"Exactly what we agreed upon."

Oh my gosh. Could this be enough evidence to arrest them? Maybe I should be recording this. I fumbled around, trying to get my phone from my purse. I wasn't sure if it would even pick up the conversation, but I had to give it a shot. Just as I pulled my phone from my bag, it rang. I was so startled that I almost tossed the phone from my hands. Pierce's number popped up. I had to take the call, but I didn't want to miss out on any of the conversation.

"Are you going to answer it?" Grammy asked.

I held the phone to my ear and whispered, "Hello."

"Are you all right, Celeste?" Pierce asked.

At least Mr. Vanderbilt was listening and could possibly tell me what was being said.

"I'm all right. Is something wrong?" I asked.

"Deidre has been arrested for the murder," Pierce announced.

I was silent, unsure of how to react.

"What's wrong?" my grandmother asked.

Clearly, she noticed something was amiss by the expression on my face. I held up my index finger, indicating that I would tell her soon.

"Are you sure?" I asked.

"Positive," Pierce answered. "I suppose they have the killer now, and everything is okay."

Did that mean that I was suspicious of Stan Knowles

and Tasha Kenmore for absolutely no reason? Something didn't add up. I wasn't buying it. It all seemed too easy. As if the police had tied Deidre up in a bow and called her the killer. All in a neat little package.

"Where are you?" Pierce asked.

Mr. Vanderbilt waved as he sat across from Stan.

"I'm eating with my grandmother," I said.

"Oh, well, I don't want to disturb you," Pierce said. "We can talk when you're finished."

"Yeah, okay," I said. "I'll call you soon."

When I ended the call, my grandmother stared at me expectantly.

"Pierce said they arrested Deidre for the murder," I whispered.

"Well, that's interesting. I guess there's no need for us to poke around any longer." Grammy's obsession with germs continued, as she pulled hand sanitizer from her pocketbook and rubbed a dab of the liquid on her hands. "Do you need some?"

I declined her offer.

"I wouldn't be so sure about not investigating, Grammy," I said, checking over my shoulder. "This doesn't seem right. I get a bad feeling about this."

"Well, if you have a bad feeling, I have a bad feeling," she said. "What do you want to do?"

"I think I should just continue with what I've been doing. Those two are up to something." I gestured over my shoulder with my thumb. "I want to find out what."

Tasha walked away from the table. I had missed their conversation, but I hoped Mr. Vanderbilt heard everything. Stan got up from the table and headed across the diner.

"Where is he going?" my grandmother asked.

When he reached the door, I said, "He's leaving."

Mr. Vanderbilt stood beside the table now.

I jumped up. "Grammy, we should go find out where he's going."

I helped my grandmother up from the table, and we hurried across the floor. Mr. Vanderbilt followed behind us.

"But what about the desserts?" he said, pointing at the display case. "You didn't get any cake."

We'd have to do that later. There was no time for chocolate. My grandmother and I hurried out the door. I didn't want to let Stan get out of my sight. When I glanced back, Tasha was watching me. Her stare sent a shiver down my spine. She knew what I was up to. Somehow, she knew. We watched as Stan got in his car.

"Grammy, you go back to the hotel. I'm going after this guy."

"I'm not letting you go alone," she said.

There was no way I was letting her drive my truck and chase. But I knew she would insist on coming with me.

"All right, but just remember I think this is a bad idea."

"I can handle myself," she said.

"We have to hurry. I don't want him to get away," I said.

"You don't want who to get away?" a snarky voice asked from behind me.

I spun around. Tasha had come out of the diner and slipped behind us. I knew she'd been suspicious of me. I didn't owe her answers, though. By the expression on her face, she wanted to punch me. No wonder her friends called her scary. She was truly scary.

"Excuse me?" my grandmother asked, placing her hands on her hips.

I knew this meant that sassy Grammy was coming out. She'd clobber Tasha with her pocketbook. Tasha just might be surprised by my spunky grandmother. She didn't take any lip off anyone.

Tasha didn't wait for an answer.

She smirked and said, "You left without ordering. Is there something wrong?"

"We changed our minds," I said.

"Yes, we saw a mouse running around in there," my grandmother said.

"Oh, that's impossible." Tasha glared.

"How is it impossible? Maybe you should ask your friend Mickey Mouse inside the diner. Apparently, he wants cheese."

Tasha continued to stare at us. Checking over my shoulder, I saw that Stan was gone. This was probably her plan all along, to stall me from being able to follow him. Well, it had worked.

"Come on, Grammy, let's go," I said as I helped her get into the truck.

Grammy and I got into the truck. Tasha stood on the sidewalk, glaring at us.

"Do you believe that woman?" Grammy asked as she buckled her seat belt.

"She's definitely involved in this," I said as I cranked the truck. "I think it's too late for us to find Stan, but we'll drive around the block until she goes back inside. Then I'll bring you back to the car."

"She's not gonna intimidate me," Grammy said with a shake of her fist.

We pulled out of the parking lot. I just hoped Tasha wasn't standing out there when we came back. I drove around the block, and sure enough, we didn't find Stan. I thought about driving over to the art gallery, but I would definitely drop Grammy off before I did that. I wasn't going to let her know my plans. I took Grammy back to the car and followed her to the hotel. I just wanted to make sure she got there okay. I thought it made her a little bit miffed at me, but I did it anyway.

I pulled into the hotel parking lot and got out of my truck. I was surprised my family was still allowed to stay here, knowing my dad and brothers. Surely they'd done something wrong by now. Broken something? It was only a matter of time. I stepped up to my mom's car.

Grammy opened the door and unbuckled her seat belt. "You're not gonna do anything that you shouldn't, are you?"

"What do you mean?" I asked innocently.

"Like snooping around somewhere without me?"

"Of course I will not snoop around without you."

Now I was completely lying. Maybe I would try to avoid snooping. No, that was impossible.

"Everything will be fine," I said.

"You'd better be telling me the truth," she warned with a wiggle of her finger.

"I'll see you soon, Grammy," I said.

She stared for a few seconds longer and got out of the truck. I watched as she walked up to the door.

When I pulled out of the parking lot, I headed right for the art gallery. I would come up with a plan as soon as I got there. As I sat at a red light, my phone rang. It was Pierce again.

"Have they released Deidre already?" I asked as I watched a woman and her black Lab cross the street.

Van would have barked fiercely if he'd seen that dog.

Pierce chuckled. "No, not quite. Apparently, they found her fingerprints on the rope. There was no other explanation of why they would be there."

"It doesn't sound like good enough evidence to me. I think they have a weak case. They might be sorry about that when it comes time for a trial."

"Well, you'll have to talk to the prosecutor about that," he said. "Did you have a nice lunch with your grandmother?"

"Sure," I said.

A white van waiting behind me at the light honked, alerting me that the light had turned green.

"There was a hesitation. What is that about?" he asked. "Was the food bad?"

Since he had called to tell me about Deidre, I probably should be honest and tell him where we'd been.

I made the next right turn. "My grandmother and I went to talk with Tasha again. I saw her talking with Stan. I think that there's something going on with those two. Stan mentioned a painting. Perhaps the stolen one."

"Maybe it has absolutely nothing to do with the murder," Pierce said.

"It just seems odd. Their behavior is weird. Plus, there was the thing I found." I got a glimpse of a Krispy Kreme shop on my left and wished I had a mouthwatering glazed doughnut.

"What thing?" he asked, snapping my attention back to the conversation.

"I went back to the scene of the crime," I said as I scooted through a yellow light.

"Of course you did," he said.

"Now, don't be negative," I said. "Remember, we're working on this together."

"If we're working together, then why are you just now telling me that?" Pierce asked.

"Because I'm just now talking to you."

He chuckled. "All right, what did you find?"

I rolled up to another red light. "A gold keychain with the initials S.K. on it. I thought that could be for Stan Knowles. But Tasha's friends call her Scary, so it could be for Scary Kenmore."

"That could be anyone's keychain," Pierce said.

"Yes, but it could be the killer's, too," I said, pushing the gas when the signal flipped to green.

"They've already arrested Deidre," he said.

"I hope they didn't make a mistake. The killer could still be out there somewhere."

"Let's hope not," he said.

"Listen, Pierce, I have to go. I'll call you back soon." I turned my truck into the art gallery's parking lot.

"What are you up to?" Pierce asked. "Your voice sounds suspicious."

"Oh, you're just saying that. How can I sound suspicious?"

I probably sounded even more suspicious when I said that. I knew I sounded as if I were up to something. Of course, I was up to something. I pulled my truck to the side of the lot. Only one other car was in the lot. It was the silver Lexus SUV I'd seen Stan driving. Pierce wouldn't be happy with me if he knew what I was up to.

"Just don't get yourself in trouble," Pierce said.

"Of course not," I said with a chuckle.

"Do not get in trouble," Pierce repeated.

I knew I sounded nervous. I always knew when the anxiety slipped through.

"I'll call you soon, okay?" I asked.

"All right," he said with a bit of hesitation.

I knew he didn't want to end the call.

"Talk to you later," I said. "I'm getting another call."

I wouldn't tell Pierce that Caleb was calling.

CHAPTER 24

Travel Trailer Tip 24:
If you can't see the driver, then the driver
can't see you. Don't stand behind the trailer
when it's in motion.

"Where are you, Celeste?" Caleb asked.

The tone of his voice sounded as if something was wrong.

"Is everything okay?" I asked, pulling my truck to the end of the lot.

"I don't know," he said.

I shoved the truck into park. "I'm driving. Now you've got me worried."

"They found that stolen painting," he said.

"Really? That's great. Where did they find it?" I asked. "Don't tell me Deidre had it."

"Someone bought it," Caleb announced.

"Interesting. Who sold it to them?" I scanned the surroundings.

An area dense with trees was next to the old school

building. The branches full of leaves added ample shade for the parking lot, but also plenty of places for someone to hide. An uneasiness tingled across my skin at the thought.

"You did," he said matter-of-factly.

In my startled state, I accidentally bumped the horn. The sound blared from the truck's hood. Oh no. What if Stan came out to find out who was honking? I had a clear view of Stan's SUV from where I sat.

"Excuse me?" I said. "I thought you said I sold the painting. But I couldn't possibly have heard that correctly."

"No, that's exactly what I said."

"I sold it?" My voice rose a decibel.

"You sold the painting. At least that's what they said."

"That's ridiculous. How would I get the painting?" I asked.

"Well, that's what I want to find out, and apparently the police will want to find out, as well, as soon as they find you." Apprehension covered his words.

"The police want me? They want to arrest me?" I asked, fanning myself with my hand. "I think I'm hyperventilating."

I'd been doing that a lot lately. Well, not actually hyperventilating, but on the edge of it.

"Okay, just calm down," he said. "We'll figure this out. I'll get you a lawyer if we have to."

"I'm going to prison. But I didn't do anything wrong." I clutched the steering wheel as if it were my life preserver.

"You won't go to prison." Caleb attempted to sound reassuring.

"Why do they think I sold the painting?" I surveyed the lot, still on high alert for any sign of Stan.

"The person said they bought it from the craft fair. The booth with that little pink-and-white trailer."

Unfortunately, I had the only pink-and-white trailer at the craft fair.

"But I didn't sell that painting," I said. "This has to be a mistake."

"Like I said, we'll figure it all out. I can meet you somewhere. Where are you?" Caleb asked.

"This is a trap. Are you working with the police?"

Caleb scoffed. "I can't believe you would say that. And I am the police."

"That means you're going to arrest me. I have to go." I ended the call.

Immediately, my phone rang again. I let Caleb's call go to my voice mail. I had to tell someone about this. I didn't want to worry my parents. Heaven knew I couldn't tell my brothers, because all they would do was laugh and start making prison jokes. Grammy would have a heart attack if I told her. Of course, that left the best person to call . . . Sammie. I dialed her number.

"Wow, am I glad you picked up right away," I said when she answered.

"Oh my goodness, what's wrong?" Sammie asked over the sound of talking in the background.

"They think I stole the painting."

"What?" She screeched into the phone.

I held it away from my ear for a second.

"Yeah, that's what I said. Caleb told me." I nervously tapped my fingers against the steering wheel.

"How would that happen?" she asked.

"Well, someone bought it from me, but I don't remember selling it. I remember all the paintings I sell. Of course I would remember, since I painted them. I'm the only one who sold my paintings."

"That's not exactly true." The tone of Sammie's voice changed.

"What do you mean?"

"I sold one of your paintings a short time ago." She rushed the words.

"You did? Which painting was it?"

"It was something unlike anything you have painted before. A portrait of an old man," she said.

"Did it have trees and greenery around him?" I asked.

"Yes, that was it," she said. "The painting wasn't that great. Oops. I just said your painting wasn't that great. I can't believe I did that."

"Don't worry about it," I said.

"No, really, I'm sorry. I shouldn't say anything like that. I usually think all your work is great. I don't know why that one just didn't appeal to me, I guess."

"That's because I didn't paint it."

Sammie asked the people in the background to be quiet and then asked, "What do you mean?"

"That was the stolen painting," I said.

"I knew you would never paint something like that." Sammie's words held more excitement. "But how was it at your booth?"

"That's what I'd like to know. I think someone might be setting me up."

I jumped a bit when movement came from the tree line. A gray cat strolled from behind a cedar tree and across the parking lot. Whew. That had sent my heart rate into a spike.

"Why would they do that? Nobody even knows you're here."

"Maybe it was because I was snooping around about the murder." I checked the time on my gold Mickey Mouse watch that my father had given me for Christmas last year.

"Yeah, but let's be real, you aren't even close to solving it," Sammie said.

"Hey," I said. "Is this pick on Celeste day? I think I was making great progress."

"Oops, there I go again," she said. "Opening my big mouth."

"Well, at least now I know how you really feel."

"Don't be mad at me," she said. "I say stupid things, you know that."

"Yes, you do."

"Hey," she said defensively.

"All right, we're getting off track here. I need to call Caleb and tell him about this. Although by the way he talked to me when he called before, it sounded as if he was already ready to visit me in prison."

"He doesn't believe you?" she asked.

"Apparently not," I said. "Maybe I should call Pierce first."

"It seems like you two have been spending a lot of time together."

"That's because he gave in and decided to work with me. Caleb has been stubborn, and so I haven't talked to him as much."

"And all this time I thought you guys were a great couple."

"I don't think we've ever been a couple," I said.

"Well, I like Pierce, too," she said.

"This doesn't have anything to do with dating," I said.

"Oh, come on, you know the chemistry is there between you and both guys. Don't try to fight it anymore."

"I'll admit that both men are smart, kind, handsome, and make me laugh, but nevertheless, I have other problems right now. I have to let you go," I said.

"Please be careful out there, Celeste, I worry about you."

"Everything will be just fine," I said.

CHAPTER 25

Travel Trailer Tip 25:
There's nothing better than sharing your
travel trailer with a dog.

After shutting off my truck, I tapped my fingers against the steering wheel and wondered what I should do next. This old school building certainly seemed eerie. Probably because it still looked abandoned, with the overgrown weeds sprouting up around the brick walls and cracks in the pavement. I couldn't just come out and ask Stan if he was the killer. He would recognize me right away if he saw me out here sitting in the truck. He would probably be suspicious if I showed up again. I could just tell him that I was an artist and interested in having my work in the gallery. Would that be such a stretch?

Yes, I'd been sneaking around with my dog and snooping in the window, but I could just tell him that I was worried about telling the truth after he caught me. Maybe he would be able to sense my nervousness, too.

Probably, but it was the only option I had right now, so I had to take a chance. I pulled the keys from the ignition and got out of the truck.

I scanned the parking lot as I walked toward the main doors. Every few seconds, I thought about turning and running back to the truck. Now that I was at the steps that led to the entrance doors, I might as well go through with this.

With shaky legs, I walked up to the doors. I couldn't believe I was doing this. My heart pounded as I opened the door and eased into the space.

A small hallway opened up into the large open space. Tables with paint cans, drop cloths, and other remodeling equipment filled the space. No one was in sight. Where was Stan? His car was in the parking lot, so I had expected to see him inside. Maybe he was with someone else . . . Tasha, perhaps? Now what would I do? I had to decide if I wanted to call out for him or just snoop around, since it appeared he wasn't here.

I'd take my chances and snoop around. Glancing to the left, I spotted a door. I supposed I could try there. What would I do if I opened the door and Stan was in that room? I would have a lot of explaining to do.

I wrapped my hand around the doorknob and twisted. It was locked. I remembered the key I had found. It was a long shot, sure, but I had to give it a try. This was the first locked door that I'd come across.

I pulled the key from my pocket and shoved it into the lock. It turned smoothly. I couldn't believe it. I'd discovered the key to the door! What was inside this room? I opened the door, hoping that no one was inside. Art supplies filled the small space. Canvases and paint. An easel with a blank canvas sat in the corner of the room. Was this Stan's art studio? A small table had papers on top. I stepped inside and walked over to it.

A notebook of sketches was open on the desk. Stan's name was signed under one of the drawings. This had to be his art studio. I knew the keychain had been Stan's. He had lost it at the crime scene. That meant that Stan really was the killer. Deidre had been arrested, but she was innocent. I had to tell someone, but I still wasn't sure if this would be enough proof. I pulled out my phone and snapped a picture of the notebook. I wasn't sure if that would do any good, but nevertheless, I'd give it a shot. As soon as I got out of here, I would call Pierce.

When I turned around to leave, Stan stood in the doorway. Terror raced through my body and shook me to my core. By the expression on his face, I knew that he wasn't happy with me. My assumption had been true that Stan was the killer. And it appeared as if I might be the next on his list. He blocked the doorway, so there was no way I would be able to get away from him. I think I let out an audible gasp. He stared at me. With a wide-legged stance and flaring nostrils, he reminded me of a bull ready to charge. We stared at each other for what seemed like forever.

His jaw tightened as he snapped, "What do you want?"

Did he recognize me? I hoped not.

"I saw the sign for the art gallery, and I'm an artist. I wanted to find information about maybe having my art here."

His deep, boisterous rumble echoed through the room. "I don't think that is possible. It's invitation only."

"How do I get an invitation?" I asked.

Now my fear had turned to anger. Why was he so

snotty? He just assumed my art wasn't good enough or maybe amateurish. Maybe it was, but he hadn't seen any of my work. How could he judge it without even seeing a painting first?

He studied my face, and I wondered if he recognized me now.

"I suppose I can see what you have to offer. Do you have any work with you?"

Why was he being nice all of a sudden?

"Why don't you come on out here, and we'll discuss it more." He motioned.

Should I fall for this? Maybe he was just being nice to lure me somewhere. But the whole purpose for me coming was to talk to him. Part of me was saying don't do it, and the other part was saying I should go.

"There's still work to be done to the building," he said.

The inside wasn't as bad as when I'd seen it last. Apparently, progress had been made. There was no art yet. I suppose he was waiting on the remodeling to be finished before adding that.

"We're still working on things, but we'll have many sections for different artists," he said, pointing across the area. "Now, let me see your work. Did you say you have some in your truck?"

I didn't have any work in my truck, but I had photos on my phone of some of my pieces. I pulled it out and scrolled through until I came to a painting of a mountain scene from back home.

"Here's one piece," I said.

He stared at the phone screen. "Oh yes, that's very lovely. Actually, I think we could use your work here."

Was he being serious? I was here investigating a killer, and now he wanted to put my work in the gallery? This was kind of exciting. Okay, I needed to get hold of myself and remember my reason for being here. Without saying another word, he snatched the phone from my hands.

"Hey, what are you doing?" I yelled.

"Don't you think I know who you are?"

Oh, I was in big trouble now. I backed away, but I only made it a couple of steps before bumping into a shelf.

"You're actually just the person I wanted to see," Stan said with an evil smile.

"Why do you want to see me?" I asked.

I was afraid of the answer.

"Oh, you have something of mine, and I want it back."

CHAPTER 26

Travel Trailer Tip 26:
Home is where you make it.

"What could I possibly have that you would want?" I asked.

I knew the answer, but I wanted him to say it out loud. I wasn't sure why, since no one would hear but me.

"I left a painting with you. I had to stash it somewhere when I took it from the mansion. And lucky you, your booth was the first one I came to. When the ditzy woman at your booth wasn't paying attention, I just put it in with your other awful paintings and no one would be the wiser. Well, maybe they would when they discovered that fantastic work of art right next to your junk."

Now he was getting me angry. What made him think he was an art critic? Just because he was trying to open an art gallery didn't mean he knew art.

"I don't know what you're talking about," I said with an unintentional sneer.

"I will just go back to your scruffy little trailer and you can get that painting for me."

"I don't have a painting at my trailer. So if you excuse me, I have to leave now." I headed toward the door, but of course he wasn't moving.

It had been worth a shot. I had to try to get out of here, but with him at the door, I didn't have a good shot.

Since I knew he wouldn't just let me walk right past him and out the door, I had to come up with an alternate plan. Maybe I needed a weapon. Unfortunately, I had nothing like that on me. I surveyed the room, trying to locate something that I might use to defend myself. The paintbrush wouldn't work. Paint? No. A canvas? Perhaps I could hit him over the head with that? But it would just break, and he would have a canvas necklace. The easel was awkward and hard to move, so that wouldn't be ideal. The longer I stood there searching for something, the more I panicked. He probably knew what I was up to, as well.

"Are you coming with me, or do I have to drag you out of here?" he asked.

This guy was despicable. I bit back a smart-aleck comment. Snark would only make matters worse, so I kept my mouth shut. I might be able to keep my mouth shut about his last question, but it didn't work for my next insult. I just couldn't help myself.

"If you're such an art critic, why are your paintings so bad?" I scrutinized the current project propped up against the easel. A weird painting of a clown smelling a daisy? File that under creepy.

"I'll have you know that someone is waiting to buy

that project." He tilted his chin upward as if extremely proud of his work.

"I hope you're not charging too much money for it. If so, they're being taken advantage of."

"Enough of your yammering. Let's go." He motioned.

"I'm not going anywhere with you." I crossed my arms in front of me.

Perhaps this wasn't the time for stubbornness.

"You don't have a choice in the matter," he said. "It wasn't a question. It was a demand."

"I don't care what you call it, I'm not going with you. End of discussion," I said.

To my left, I spotted a can of paint thinner on the table. Maybe if I grabbed that and splashed it on him, he would be distracted. After that, I could run out of the room. But even so, it wouldn't keep him busy for long.

What would I do when I got into the other area? I had to make a run for the door. If I got outside, I might stand a better chance of making it all the way to my truck. Unless, of course, he had locked the front doors. There was no way for me to know until I got there. If they were locked, it would be too late to do anything else. As it was right now, I had little chance in this room. Distraction was my only option. I'd have to give it a shot. My movements would have to be fast.

"You hid the stolen painting. They want to arrest me for that," I said with anger in my voice.

"That's none of my concern," he said.

"How did you steal that art from the mansion?" I asked.

"I had a little help," he said with an evil smile. "Ellen was in on the plot with me."

Ellen was helping him steal the expensive painting? I should have suspected something like that was happening, since the clues were right in front of my face.

"Why did you kill her?" I asked.

The reality of my situation sent a shiver down my spine. The killer was right in front of me. I knew he wanted to make me his next victim.

Stan shrugged. "I suppose I got greedy and wanted everything for myself. When Ellen said she would confess to what we'd planned, I lost control."

In a fit of rage, he killed Ellen? As if I wasn't terrified enough before hearing him confess, now I was petrified.

I needed to cause a distraction right now. However, he wasn't taking his eyes off me. I would just have to make a move for it. As if fate had stepped in, a noise sounded from somewhere behind him. He glanced over his shoulder. As I reached for the paint thinner, a movement caught my attention, and *I* became distracted. I saw the top of a tiny gray-haired head outside the window. Grammy? I really hoped my eyes were deceiving me. Unfortunately, running over and checking out the window wasn't an option. I turned my attention back to the doorway, just as he did. I hoped he didn't see Grammy. What was she doing here?

I had lost my chance at grabbing the paint thinner. The frown on Stan's face let me know that his patience had worn thin. He flared his nostrils and moved toward me. I backed up a couple of steps.

He reached out and wrapped his hands around my arms. "You're coming with me. We're going to get the painting."

"All right, all right," I said as I struggled to get away

from him. "You don't have to grab me so hard. If I take you to the painting, will you let me go?"

He didn't answer. I knew that meant that he had no intention of letting me go, even after I gave him the painting. Giving him the painting wasn't even an option, since Sammie had sold it. When he found out, I would be a goner. I would have to stall long enough to get away. Just being out of this tiny room would help my claustrophobia.

He dragged me across the hard floor.

"Let go," I yelled.

Movement caught my attention. My grandmother's little face was sticking up to the glass. Stan hadn't noticed her. At that second, Grammy turned, and our gazes met. Her mouth moved. She was saying something. Her voice was muted by the glass. I was glad there was no sound, because I didn't want Stan to discover her. He would do something to her if he caught her.

Maybe now she'd call the police. Grammy darted away from the window. I just hoped that she stayed away. I had to keep Stan stalled long enough for the police to arrive. I didn't want to get in a vehicle with him, because there was no telling where he would take me and leave me. They'd never find me.

I managed to get my arm free. It did no good, though, because he just grabbed it again.

"Don't think you're getting away," he yelled.

"Where are you taking me?"

"To get that painting."

"I told you I would. You don't have to drag me across this floor. You're hurting me."

"You already put up a fight. I'm not playing any games with you. I'm not taking chances."

Movement caught my attention again. This time, my brother Stevie was peeking in the window. Oh, this was bad. I knew something was about to happen, because there was no way Stevie would wait for the police to arrive. He had a temper when it came to people messing with his family. Stan was about to encounter Stevie's wrath.

I just hoped that Stan didn't hurt my brother. Stevie must have driven my grandmother here. I wasn't sure how they found me, but nevertheless, I was glad and scared at the same time. If something happened to them, I would never forgive myself. It would be my fault that I put them in this situation. We were almost at the hallway that led to the main door now.

"I really don't want to be scraped across the ground outside," I said.

"Well, I want a lot of things, but that doesn't mean I'm going to get them. One thing I know for sure, I'm getting that painting. So no more lip out of you."

"You think you're such a tough guy," I said.

He was about to learn otherwise.

"Yeah, well, you think you're so tough," he said. "I guess I showed you."

He pulled me down the hallway toward the door. I expected Stevie to burst through at any time. What if Stan had a gun? I couldn't stand the thought of something happening to my brother.

"Who was that?" Stan asked with a bit of panic in his voice. "Did you call the police?"

Had the police arrived? Would I be saved, or would Stan hold me hostage inside with the police surrounding the building? Situations like that rarely ended well for the hostage.

"I didn't call the police," I said. "How would I do that when you practically have me in a choke hold?"

"That's a bit of an exaggeration, don't you think?" Stan asked. "I saw someone gazing in that back window. The person resembled you, only about twenty-five years older."

My mother? Oh no. Was my whole family here? Actually, that wouldn't surprise me in the least. I was shocked they hadn't stormed the building already.

"Maybe you're imagining things," I said.

"I have a feeling you are up to something." Stan pulled me across the floor again.

We headed toward the back windows. Once by the window, Stan peered outside, searching for whomever had been lurking outside. I sure hoped my mother didn't pop up again. It had to have been her. I mean, she fit that description perfectly. Movement came at the front door. I spotted my grandma, my mother, my father, Stevie, and Hank.

Based on their hand gestures, they indicated that they planned to sneak in and hide. I sure hoped they knew what they were doing. Did they call the police? Perhaps this would be a better job for law enforcement. Did they call Caleb or Pierce? Someone had to get me out of here. Surely Stan would get tired of holding me soon and let go. Could I convince him to let go? Nope. Been there, done that.

"You're really hurting my arms," I said.

"Too bad," he snapped.

"Why are you so mean?" I asked. "Have you always been this nasty?"

"Yes, I have been told I've always been despicable." His voice was filled with laughter.

"Why do you sound so happy about that?"

"I wear it with pride," he said matter-of-factly.

"Clearly there's no one out here," I said. "Why don't we go ahead and get in my truck, and I'll drive you to the painting."

"I saw someone messing around back there. She looked just like you. I suppose this is someone you know."

"I don't know what you're talking about," I said.

He wouldn't get answers out of me. After another minute of standing by the window, Stan dragged me like a rag doll back across the floor, headed toward the front doors. Anxiety pulsed through my body as I contemplated what would happen when Stan took me outside. With my family reunion waiting out there, surely they could overcome him. Unless he had another trick up his paint-smock sleeve.

Mr. Vanderbilt appeared in front of the doors, standing on the outside. He gave me a thumbs-up. What was he doing? Stan tried to open the doors, but they wouldn't budge. A flagpole on the front steps had toppled over and landed in front of the door, acting as a barricade. The object had been a relic from the former school. How had this happened?

Mr. Vanderbilt appeared in front of the door with a wide smile on his face. "I managed to knock that flagpole over. It took a lot of energy, but I did it."

I wanted out of the building, not to stay inside. Mr. Vanderbilt must be completely confused.

"No, Mr. Vanderbilt, open the doors," I yelled.

Stan glared at me. "What are you talking about?"

"There's a ghost. He blocked the doors with that flagpole."

"You're crazy," he said.

"How else can you explain that the doors won't open?" I smirked.

"The wind knocked over the flagpole," he said in a snarky tone.

"You'll see," I said.

"Mr. Vanderbilt, open the door."

I could've used Mr. Vanderbilt's help earlier when was I inside that room. Maybe he could've thrown something at Stan. Now he was holding me inside.

After a couple of seconds, Mr. Vanderbilt's eyes widened, as if it had dawned on him that he had blocked the doors when he really should open them. He closed his eyes, focusing on the flagpole. The flagpole scooted away from the doors' handle and fell to the ground with a clank. With a smug smile on his face, Mr. Vanderbilt stepped out of the way. Stan tumbled forward, spilling outside and falling onto the front steps. He had pushed his body against the door trying to get it open. I took this opportunity to run right out the door. At the same time, my family pounced on Stan, and punches commenced. They really were letting him have it.

I dialed 911. It didn't matter, because the police were rolling into the parking lot before I could hit the second 1. Sirens blared, and lights flashed. My family continued smacking Stan. Grammy even hit him over his head with her pocketbook. A can of green beans rolled across the pavement.

"You had green beans in your purse, Grammy?" I asked.

"You never know when you might get hungry," she answered.

Mr. Vanderbilt was standing to the side, laughing at the scene. It was kind of funny to see Grammy hitting Stan with that big brown pocketbook.

The police jumped out of their cars and over to the melee. They managed to get Stan out from under my family. He appeared relieved to be going to jail. It was probably better than being attacked by my clan. My mother and grandmother ran over to me.

"Are you all right, dear?" Grammy asked.

"I'm fine. How are you all? What a relief that you don't have black eyes."

"The only one going to have black eyes is that despicable man right there." Grammy pointed at Stan as he was being guided in handcuffs toward a police car.

I spotted Pierce and Caleb walking together toward us. This would certainly be one heck of a story to recount. How would I get out the whole thing and how it went down? My favorite part was Grammy and her pocketbook. But thank heavens I got away from Stan before he'd gotten the chance to kill me, too.

Caleb and Pierce walked up to me.

"Is everything all right here?" Caleb asked.

"Oh, it's just peachy now," I said. "What are you guys doing together?"

"Hey, we work together," Pierce said.

"I don't know if you work together or against each other," I said.

"Well, this time we worked together," Caleb said.

"What's that mean?" I asked.

"We found the painting and got it back," Pierce said.

"All while you found the killer," Caleb said.

"I'm not so sure if I found the killer, or the killer found me," I confessed.

"I still think I was right. You shouldn't have gotten into such a dangerous situation," Caleb said.

"I think I was right. We worked together, and we found a killer," Pierce said.

They were still arguing. I didn't think they would ever agree on anything. Well, I supposed they had agreed on finding a painting. Maybe that was progress.

Stevie and Hank walked up. Oh no. How were they going to embarrass me this time?

"Which one of you is dating my sister?" Stevie asked.

Yes, that was definitely an embarrassing question.

"Hey, I think Mom needs you," I said, shooing them away.

"No, she's good," Stevie said.

Stevie and Hank turned back to Pierce and Caleb, waiting for an answer. I didn't know that I was dating Caleb or Pierce. I wouldn't consider a few dates actually boyfriend/girlfriend status. However, I knew at some point I would have to make a decision, because based on the stares I got from Pierce and Caleb right now, I knew that they wanted an answer, as well.

"Well, you can't put Celeste on the spot like that," Pierce said.

He winked at me. I really appreciated that save.

After a few more seconds, Hank said, "Just let us know so that we can have a talk with him."

I shook my head as the guys walked away.

"Sorry about that," I said.

"Like I said, they shouldn't put you on the spot. Although . . ." Pierce said.

"We would like to know," Caleb said.

"I don't think I can talk about this right now," I said.

"Sorry, that's understandable. You have been through

a lot," Caleb said. "Pierce and I were talking while in the car together."

"I was the topic of discussion while I was being held hostage?"

"You know we would've been here if we'd known," Pierce said.

"I know you would've been here. You guys helped me more than you probably should have, considering I got us all into dangerous situations. I guess I have a knack for it," I said with a shrug.

"You certainly have a knack for solving crime," Pierce said.

"Oh, one more thing," Caleb said. "When we went by your trailer, we found a painting outside the door. Sammie said it was haunted, and she wanted us to take it with us."

"What?" I had a feeling I knew which painting he meant. I'd been so busy solving the murder that I hadn't thought of the woman's portrait since I'd painted it.

Caleb walked over to Pierce's car and pulled out the canvas. Before he even made it back over, Mr. Vanderbilt popped up beside me.

Caleb showed us the painting. "This is the one."

"Why did she say it was haunted?" Pierce asked.

"Because I suspect that it is," I said.

Mr. Vanderbilt was transfixed on the painting.

"She's breathtaking," he said.

So far, the woman hadn't popped through from the spirit world. That didn't mean it wouldn't happen all of a sudden, or maybe when I least expected it.

"Laura Nally is her name," said the ghost. "She is my wife. My name is Nathaniel Nally, and I was a caretaker at the Biltmore Estate. I'm not Mr. Vanderbilt."

That all made sense now. A heaviness came over the area. Right before my eyes, the woman appeared next to Mr. Vanderbilt. Or should I say Nathaniel Nally? Laura took Nathaniel's hand, and they walked away from us. Soon, a bright light came from around the side of the building. Mr. and Mrs. Nally followed that light as if it were pulling them in that direction.

My heart danced with delight that they were together now. It all happened so quickly. Mrs. Nally had returned to guide her husband to the light. Mr. Nathaniel Nally had come through in the painting, and now was free to move on from this dimension. Pierce and Caleb had no clue what had just happened. Too bad I hadn't gotten the chance to say goodbye.

"We should get back to the craft fair," I said.

This fair would be over soon. While it had started with tragedy, at least something good had come from my trip to the Biltmore. Mr. Nally had moved on, and Ellen's killer had been caught. The next craft fair was calling my name. Would there be more mysteries to solve? I hoped not, but if there were, I was ready for the task.

ACKNOWLEDGMENTS

Many thanks to my family and friends. They embrace my quirkiness. Love you all! Also, thank you to my editor, Michaela Hamilton, and my agent, Jill Marsal.

Don't miss the next irresistible Haunted Craft Fair
mystery by Rose Pressey

MURDER CAN FROST YOUR DOUGHNUT

Coming soon from Kensington Publishing Corp.

Keep reading to enjoy a taste!

CHAPTER 1

The last rays of sunset faded to a deep navy blue as evening approached the Sevier County Fair. A late summer breeze ruffled the leaves of nearby oak trees. Lights appeared on the Ferris wheel and carousel, waiting for the nighttime riders. Carnies yelled as I strolled by the ring toss. Memories of attending the fair with my parents floated back. That had been twenty-some years ago. My father always won me a stuffed animal. He was the best at shooting the little ducks with the water gun. I missed those simpler times.

Not that my family wouldn't be here tonight. Soon, my parents and brothers would arrive from nearby Gatlinburg. That meant my best friend Samantha Sutton and I would only have a short time until the chaos ensued. My father and brothers tended to be unknowingly mischievous. They were basically walking disasters. I'd thought about attaching caution signs to their backs. As long as I kept them from the hazardous things around the fair, I figured things would work out all right. Though I suppose for them, all things were hazardous.

Keeping them out of trouble was a full-time job. My mother knew that all too well. She'd been shepherding my dad and brothers out of potentially perilous situations for years. It was a wonder her hair hadn't fully turned gray by now. She still had dark hair like me. I described the shade as night sky with touches of walnut mixed in. Those were two of my favorite paint colors that I liked to use. Everyone commented on how much my mom and I looked alike. Just like me at a little over five feet tall, she packed a powerful punch.

The smells of deep fryers and manure drifted through the air to the midway, where I was strolling with my best friend, Sammie. It was an odd aroma, for sure, and not appetizing at all. Yet that didn't stop people from indulging in the deep-fried butter and deep-fried candy bars. The hum of the machinery from the nearby Tilt-A-Whirl made it difficult to hear my best friend.

"Is it just me or does that man look just like Johnny Cash?" Sammie asked, louder this time, as the man walked by us.

The loud tinkling of the Ferris wheel as it went round and round made it hard to hear. Sammie and I stood by the fence at the edge of the ride. We'd turned our attention away from the ride to the passersby. Couples strolled hand in hand. Parents tried to calm their excited children down from their cotton-candy high.

Sammie was the opposite of me in the looks department. She was tall, with blond hair the shade of a glass of bubbling champagne. In the past six months, she'd grown out her locks a bit, but they were still styled in a bouncy bob.

"Oh, it's not just you. He looks like Johnny Cash, all right. He's here for the celebrity impersonation contest."

I turned my attention to a red balloon that floated skyward. Someone would be upset that they'd lost it. With so much activity, taking in every detail of my surroundings proved difficult. Being an artist meant I liked to study things. The habit came in handy when I wanted to paint from memory. Plus, it was useful when being questioned by the police. Trouble seemed to follow me lately. I hoped that was all behind me now. The police part, not the painting.

"Really? Who else is here? Maybe I can get some autographs." Sammie wiggled her eyebrows.

"All the iconic country stars. Johnny Cash, Patsy Cline, Loretta Lynn, Dolly Parton, and even Elvis Presley." I ticked the list off on my fingers.

"Oh, Elvis? You know I love Elvis." Sammie fanned herself.

"Who doesn't?"

"Young or old?" she asked.

"Both," I said with a smile.

"Even better. I love both," she said. "So, there's like a big contest for the impersonators?"

"Yes, it's held at the end of the fair, but they have other shows leading up to that. One of them is tonight, I think."

"Okay, now I'm on the lookout for Elvis." Sammie scanned the crowd.

Yes, the county fair was in full swing. Not only were there rides, games, and plenty of bad food to eat, but there was an arts and crafts fair, too. I had set up a booth, hoping to sell some of my paintings.

Last year, I'd become a full-time artist, and although it had been rocky at times, things were going well now. I had no idea becoming an artist could have such an interesting start. Not to mention, I had no idea that I had more than just a talent for painting. Apparently, I had some kind of psychic ability that came out through my art. I knew that sounded weird, but it was true. Ghosts tended to appear when I unknowingly painted them.

At first, I hadn't believed my eyes. I thought maybe I had been losing my mind. Not until I'd spoken with the ghosts had I accepted what was happening. Sammie had seen the spirits, as had a few other people, too. At least I knew it wasn't just me witnessing the crazy things.

At first, Sammie had been reluctant to come with me to the fair. She said all the food was too tempting, and she hated dealing with the mosquitoes. But I'd convinced her to make the trip and look around the midway before the arts and crafts fair section opened tomorrow.

Somehow, I'd also talked her into joining me and just watching as others took a spin on some of the rides. I'd told her maybe I'd ride the Ferris wheel, but I wasn't much for thrill-taking. I liked to play it safe. People would say that wasn't true based on some of the scrapes I got into. Like I said, trouble found me. I didn't go out searching for it. I mean, these things truly found me. I had ghosts telling me that they could help me solve murders, so the way I saw things, it was my duty to look into the crimes.

Sammie wasn't the only one with me tonight. In my arms was Van. Or, to give his full name, Vincent Van Gogh. My tiny white Chihuahua had been my sidekick since I'd discovered him at the shelter. When our eyes met, it had been love at first sight. We'd been inseparable ever since. He'd gotten his name because of his one floppy ear. It seemed like an appropriate moniker.

Sometimes Van liked to walk on his leash, but right now, I held him in my arms, because he'd gotten tired from all the excitement. Plus, he loved being snuggled up next to me. I enjoyed the cuddling just as much. We were like two peas in a pod. I suspected he'd perk up when we neared the corn dog vendor.

"Oh, look, there are the candy apples." Sammie pointed. "I can't believe I let you talk me into this."

"I want caramel with nuts." I sounded like a kid again.

Sammie and I approached the stand that sold the apples, cotton candy, and pretzels. It would be hard to walk away with just one. The junk food aroma wafted through the air, making my stomach rumble to attention.

I'd just paid for my apple when Sammie said, "Don't look now, but your family's here."

"What?" I said. "They weren't supposed to be here until tomorrow."

"I guess they changed their minds," she said with a grimace.

I loved my family dearly, but if trouble followed me, then double trouble followed them. Chaos trailed along with them like a tornado swirling across the sky, destroying everything in its path. The fair wouldn't know what hit when they got through with it.

"Have they seen us yet?" I asked, trying to hide behind a tall, bald-headed man next to me in line.

The man pinched his eyebrows together and moved up a couple of steps.

"Oh, you know you're not going to be able to hide from them," Sammie said. "Plus, yes, they've seen us. They're practically running toward us. Bless their hearts."

I turned around and made eye contact with my mother. She gave a half-hearted wave, as if to apologize. My brother Stevie accidentally knocked over a trash can as he lumbered toward me. Hank plodded along beside Stevie. They were carbon copies of my dad. Average height, but solidly built like wrecking balls. Their dark hair hadn't grayed like my father's yet, but if they kept up their frantic pace, it probably wouldn't be long. Either that, or they'd turn my hair gray. Maybe both.

My brothers saw nothing in front of them, because they focused on one thing at a time. Right now, that one thing was me. They looked like babies learning to walk for the first time as they bounded toward me. Sammie and I stared at my family, unable to take our eyes off them.

"Only one trash can down. Not too bad," Sammie said, taking a bite of her apple.

"Let's step away from the food stand in case they crash into it," I said.

"Good thinking," Sammie said around a laugh.

Sammie and I walked toward them. Van wiggled in my arms, deciding he wanted down again. I placed him on the ground, and he trotted along beside me on his leash. When my family neared us, my dad's mouth tilted to one side in his signature grin, but then he headed toward the food stand like a bloodhound sniffing out a clue. My mother hurried after him.

"Eddie, where do you think you're going?" she yelled. "No, you don't need a corn dog. You just had supper."

No doubt he'd get the corn dog anyway, and probably a couple of other things in the process. I supposed tonight would be okay, just this once, as long as he was good on his healthy eating plan for the rest of the week. My mom had her hands full between watching after my dad and my brothers.

"How's it going, Sis?" my brother Stevie asked.

"Just checking out the fair, guys. What are y'all into? Staying out of trouble, I hope. Not destroying anything?"

That was more of a plea than a question. They didn't catch the hint, though.

"Hey, what does that mean? You're always thinking the worst, aren't you? Don't be so negative." The small scar above Hank's lip became more noticeable when he snarled. He'd bitten an electrical cord as a baby. My mother claimed that had given him a special talent at fixing electronics.

"What's up, Sammie?" Stevie studied his boots as if he were somehow suddenly bashful.

When Sammie flashed her perfect smile, Hank winked at her, and Stevie shoved him. They'd always had a thing for Sammie. I'd cautioned her not to get involved with dating either one. Not that they weren't sweet and great brothers, but I wasn't sure Sammie was the best match for either one.

"We're here for the celebrity impersonation show. Mom and Dad want to see it," Stevie said.

"When does it start?" I asked and then took a bite of my apple. Nuts that had been stuck to the caramel dropped onto my T-shirt.

"In about five minutes. Are you going?" Stevie asked, though his attention was focused on Sammie.

After brushing the crumbs from my shirt, I turned to Sammie. "What do you say? Should we watch the show with this bunch?"

She finished her bite of apple, and then said, "Sure, why not?"

"Who performs first?" I asked.

Stevie shrugged his muscular shoulders. "I don't know for sure, maybe Patsy Cline. There's a big Elvis grand finale."

"Oh, I'm most looking forward to Elvis," I said excitedly.

"Who isn't?" Sammie said, practically swooning.

"You like Elvis, Sammie? I do a good Elvis impersonation." Stevie swayed his hips.

I groaned. "Please don't ever do that again."

Stevie and Hank spoke to a couple of people they knew.

"I have to hand it to them. Your brothers like to have a good time." Sammie tossed the remainder of her candy apple into the nearby trash can.

"Don't remind me," I said.

After my mother and father joined us, we headed toward the stage to watch the show. My dad, of course, had a giant corn dog with mustard slathered over it. Not only had he gotten the corn dog, but he'd managed to finagle the jumbo-sized one that they had advertised on the poster in front of the concession stand.

"I see dad won the battle," I said as my mother walked beside me.

Van wagged his tail as my mom scratched behind his ears.

"I told him that's the only one for today," she said.

I raised an eyebrow. "The only one corn dog or the only one treat?"

"That one corn dog is the only treat he's getting, of course," she said without confidence.

I knew that he wouldn't pay attention to her. My father had diabetes and other health issues, so my mother was always after him to watch what he ate. Tonight, she would have a battle on her hands. There was just too much temptation.

I was torn between wanting him to be happy, getting what he wanted, and wanting him to be healthy and stick around with us longer. I didn't want to lose him. I looked over and saw how happy my father was as he walked along with his family, enjoying his corn dog. I suppose I was a lot like him. Everyone said I was just like my mother. Of course, we looked alike, with the same dark hair and eyes, but I had a lot of my father's traits, too. Without a doubt, I had my quirky moments.

My family and I gathered in front of the stage. A large banner announced the FIFTH ANNUAL MUSIC LEGENDS TRIBUTE CONTEST. My brothers fought over who would stand next to Sammie. Ultimately, they figured out one could stand on each side of her. Speakers flanked the front of the stage, with multi-colored spotlights shining toward where the performers would stand. Other lights shone out into the crowd. The sky had turned completely dark, with a million stars twinkling in the black expanse. The temperature was perfect for the event at a pleasant seventy degrees. A microphone was in the middle of the stage, waiting for a performer to take stage. People were crammed together, waiting for the action to start.

A warm, gentle breeze carried across the crowd. Even with the perfect conditions, a sense of uneasiness fell over me. What was wrong? Why did I feel so antsy? The evening had been perfect so far. I had to shake off the feeling. Nothing would bother me as soon as the show started. At least, that was what I tried to tell myself. So why was it not working? Why did the feeling remain?

Movement caught my attention. At the corner of the stage, I saw a shadowy figure moving away from the area. I couldn't quite make out what the person was doing, but something about their actions seemed suspicious to me. As if they were sneaking around, specifically trying not to be caught. Why would they do that? I contemplated walking over there to see what they were doing, but I reminded myself to stay out of trouble. Whatever they were doing was none of my business. They were probably just setting up equipment for tonight's performance. I watched the area for several more seconds to see if the person returned, but they had disappeared from sight. I turned my attention back to the stage. No need to worry, I reminded myself.

Band members filed onto the stage and picked up instruments. More lighting lit up the dark sky. Even more people had gathered around, waiting for the show to start. After a couple more minutes, Patsy Cline stepped on the stage. Well, not the real Patsy, of course, but an impressive look-alike. She opened her mouth, and the melodic lyrics flowed. She sang one of my favorite songs, "Why Can't He Be You." My mom and dad held hands as they swayed to the music.

Sammie poked me in the side and then pointed toward the backstage area. "It's Elvis."

I only caught a glimpse, but just the sight of the impersonator made me swoon a bit.

"It's Johnny Cash over there." Stevie pointed toward the man dressed in black.

Wow, celebrities were everywhere. We enjoyed several more songs from Patsy. She was singing "Sweet Dreams" now. Since Elvis wasn't due to hit the stage for another twenty minutes, I decided to take Van to my trailer. He was probably hungry and tired.

"I'm taking Van back to the trailer for his nap, Mom. I'll be back in just a few minutes."

She nodded. "Just be careful."

My mother always said that, no matter if I was going two steps away or cross-country. It was just her thing, I guess. Another one of her quirks. We all had them.

I headed out across the green lawn toward my pink Shasta trailer. It would be my home away from home during a craft fair. I rolled up to each venue with my pink Ford F-1 towing the tiny trailer. Both were my pride and joy. What could I say? I loved pink. Plus, it was kind of hard for me to go unnoticed with my pink mobile art studio. Everyone would remember me.

During the day, nearby wildflowers added bursts of color, but the dark of night concealed the blooms. A pale crescent moon slipped in and out of view. Music and cheers drifted across the wind. A rustling noise came from my right. Van barked. I turned my attention toward the nearby wooded area.

"Hello?" I called.

No one replied. With no other sounds, I continued toward my destination. I'd already parked my truck and trailer at the spot where I would set up my booth for the next three days. With everything mostly ready for the festivities starting tomorrow, I only needed to set up my canvases in the morning. Things would start bright and early. Surprisingly, I was a morning person, so I didn't mind being up before sunrise.

Other vendors had set up their trailers for the sale, with most of them putting up tables and signage tonight in preparation for the event. Probably so they could sleep in just a bit longer in the morning. They weren't the only ones with trailers around. I knew some of the other fair staff had places to stay around here, too. Like some of the celebrity impersonators. Maybe I'd run into some of them. My mom would love it if I snapped pictures of some of them.

After just a short distance more, I spotted an Elvis impersonator coming out of a trailer. He stopped at the door and looked around, as if he were trying to see if anyone watched him. For some reason, this made me hesitate. I thought he was acting kind of strange. Not wanting him to see me, I moved over to a nearby oak tree.

With Van in my arms, I hid behind the trunk, peeking around the edge. Unfortunately, it was too far to get a look at the man's face. All I saw was the white bejeweled jumpsuit and his dark hair. Was he wearing a wig? After a few more seconds of looking around, the Elvis impersonator hurried away from the trailer.

"That was odd, Van," I said.

He barked as if he knew exactly what I'd said. I shook off the uneasy feeling and continued across the way toward my trailer. As I passed the trailer that the Elvis impersonator had stepped out of, another strange vibe came over me. I brushed that off, too. It was probably just anxiety from the upcoming show. Or was it?

When I reached the trailer, that creepy feeling clung to me like lint on Johnny Cash's black pants. Right away, I saw that the trailer's door was slightly ajar. Maybe the wind had blown it open? Van's ears perked, and he growled, sending out his telltale warning. However, the closer I got, the more I realized what I was looking at.

A man dressed in a gold suit lay on the trailer floor. Was he alive? I used my phone to shine light on the scene. Whether the man was dead or not, the circumstances surprised me. With a wire wrapped around his neck, he still clutched a doughnut in his right hand.

Connect with Us

Visit us online at
KensingtonBooks.com
to read more from your favorite authors, see books
by series, view reading group guides, and more.

for sneak peeks, chances to win books and prize packs,
and to share your thoughts with other readers.

facebook.com/kensingtonpublishing
twitter.com/kensingtonbooks

Tell us what you think!

To share your thoughts, submit a review,
or sign up for our eNewsletters, please visit:
KensingtonBooks.com/TellUs.